PEOPLE LIKE US

PEOPLE LIKE US

A NOVEL

LISA DALE

People Like Us is a work of fiction. All incidents and dialogue, and all characters with the exception of some historical and public figures, are products of the author's imagination. Where real-life figures appear, the situations, incidents and dialogues concerning those persons are fictional. Names, characters, places and incidents are either the products of the author's imagination or are used fictitiously. In all other respects, any resemblance to persons living or dead is entirely coincidental.

Editing by Laurie Gibson
Author Photo by George Dale
Cover and layout design by Golden Ratio Book Design

Published by Mu Publishing

First Edition
ISBN (print): 978-1-7347896-2-1
ISBN (e-book): 978-1-7347896-3-8

For
The People of Palestine

PALESTINE

A 100-Year Potted History

1917-1918: Palestine passes from Ottoman to British rule. The British Government issues a statement, known as the **Balfour Declaration**, announcing its support for the establishment of a 'national home for the Jewish people' in Palestine.

1933-1945: Jewish immigration, encouraged by the Balfour principles and fuelled by people seeking refuge from **Hitler's Nazi Germany**, brings about a tenfold increase in the Jewish population of Palestine.

29 November 1947: The UN General assembly adopts the **United Nations Partition Plan for Palestine**, which proposes to divide Palestine into an Arab state and a Jewish state, and to place Jerusalem under a Special International Regime. Arab Palestinians reject the plan because, despite owning 93% of the land and making up two-thirds of the population, the plan allocates to them less than 50% of the land.

30 November 1947: The first deaths of the **1947–49 Palestine War** occur during an ambush of two buses carrying Jews.

14 May 1948: The **British Mandate for Palestine** ends and the Jews declare an independent **State of Israel** over 78% of Palestine, leaving only Gaza and West Bank as Palestine.

15 May 1948: An Arab coalition enters the region and the civil war transforms into a wider Israeli/Arab war. During ten months of fighting, around 700,000 Palestinian Arabs flee or are expelled from their homes in the area that becomes Israel, and they become Palestinian refugees. Israel calls it the **War of Independence**. Palestinians call it **Al-Nakba** ('the Catastrophe').

11 May 1949: The UN General Assembly adopts a resolution to admit the State of Israel to membership in the United Nations.

10 October 1959: The **Fatah Party** is founded by **Yasser Arafat**.

1965: The **Palestine Liberation Organisation** (PLO) is formed under the leadership of Yasser Arafat.

5-10 June 1967: **The Six Day War** sees Israel capture the West Bank and East Jerusalem from Jordan, Gaza and the Sinai Peninsular from Egypt, and Golan Heights from Syria.

6-25 October 1973: The **Yom Kippur War** sees Egyptian and Syrian forces invading the Sinai Peninsular and Golan

Heights respectively, in an ultimately failed attempt to reclaim territory from the Israelis.

1978: The **Camp David Accords** result in Israel returning Sinai to Egypt.

December 1987-September 1993: The period of the **First Intifada** sees Palestinians in West Bank and Gaza protesting against continued Israeli occupation and oppression.

1988: A meeting of the Palestinian National Council in Algiers adopts the idea of a **two-state solution** (an independent State of Palestine alongside the State of Israel) and recognises the UN's 1947 Partition Plan.

1991: Israel stops the free movement of Palestinians between Gaza, Israel and the West Bank and requires Palestinians to hold permits to enter Israel.

September 1993: **Oslo Accord I** is signed at The White House by Israeli Prime Minister Yitzhak Rabin and PLO negotiator Mahmoud Abbas containing mutual recognition of the State of Israel and the proposed **Palestinian Authority** (PA). This marks the start of a failed seven year on-and-off period of negotiations towards a final peace treaty between Israel and Palestine.

1994: The Palestinian Authority (PA) is established as a consequence of Oslo Accord I. Israel withdraws troops from Gaza towns and from Jericho. It builds a perimeter fence around Gaza and starts to exercise total control in and out.

1994: The **Nobel Peace Prize** is awarded to Israeli Prime Minister Yitzak Rabin, Israeli Foreign Minister Shimon Peres and PLO Chairman Yasser Arafat.

September 1995: **Oslo Accord II** is signed in Taba (in the Sinai Peninsula, Egypt) by Israeli Prime Minister Yitzhak Rabin and PLO Chairman Yasser Arafat. This divides the West Bank (except Hebron) into **Areas A, B and C**. (Area A: 18% of the West Bank, Palestinians only, the main towns, under PA control; Area B: 22% of the West Bank, Palestinians only, scattered villages, under Israeli/ PA joint control; Area C: 60% of the West Bank, under Israeli control and use (settlements, military zones, future expansion)).

4 November 1995: Israeli Prime Minister Yitzak Rabin is assassinated at the Kings of Israel Square, Tel Aviv by an Israeli ultranationalist who opposes the Oslo Accords peace process.

11-25 July 2000: With the Oslo Accords peace process stalled, this **Camp David Summit** between US President Bill Clinton, Israeli Prime Minister Ehud Barak and PA Chairman Yasser Arafat fails to reach any fresh agreement on the way ahead.

September 2000-February 2005: The period of the **Second Intifada** sees Palestinians in West Bank and Gaza again protesting against continued Israeli occupation and oppression.

2002: The Israelis commence construction of the 'separation barrier' (**Apartheid Wall**), a 708-kilometre physical barrier along the Israel/West Bank border.

2004: Israel withdraws from Gaza entirely.

2007: **Hamas** takes power in Gaza, and Israel establishes a land, air and sea blockade that continues to today.

2020: The USA brokers peace deals between Israel and a number of Arab states (the United Arab Emirates (UAE), Bahrain, Sudan and Morocco) which sees the latter officially recognise Israel for the first time and the 'normalization' of relations between them.

The Palestine question, however, remains unresolved…

These soldiers of peace recognise that the world we live in is rising above the trappings of religious and racial hatred and conflict. They recognise that the spurning of agreements reached in good faith and the forceful occupation of land can only fan the flames of conflict. They know from their own experience that, it is in a situation such as this, that extremists on all sides thrive, fed by the blood lust of centuries gone by.

These Palestinian and Israeli campaigners for peace know that security for any nation is not abstract; neither is it exclusive. It depends on the security of others; it depends on mutual respect and trust. Indeed, these soldiers of peace know that their destiny is bound together, and that none can be at peace while others wallow in poverty and insecurity.

–President Nelson Mandela
on the occasion of the International Day of Solidarity with the Palestinian People, December 4th 1997

1

Hassan

Present Day – Visiting the Bubble

Two hundred and thirty thousand people! Why on earth does he put himself through this each year? Hassan closes his eyes, inhales, searches for the words.

Sixteen years ago, three Palestinians met with three Israelis in a hotel just outside Bethlehem. Each one of us was on edge, wondering what to expect. Armed with not even an escape plan, we Palestinians had invited the enemy to sit with us. We had to be crazy after everything that had happened! My two pals said our friends and families would never speak to us again when they learned of it, and that was their best-case scenario. My biggest fear that day? That I was dishonouring my dead brother's memory. I can't speak for the Israelis, but I suspect they believed they were about to be taken hostage.

The dog, sitting by Hassan's side, stands up and wanders out of the kitchen. She's heard it all before. "Thanks for the support!" Hassan calls after the retreating figure. "I should put you back in that cardboard box and return you to the construction site where I found you." It's a lame threat, as they both know.

He'll talk about his run-ins with Israeli soldiers on the streets of his youth, and what happened to his brother, and why he convened that meeting back in 2006. He hopes his words tonight will reach more people, open more minds.

Hassan rinses his mug in the sink and upturns it on the draining board. He goes to scratch his chin expecting to find a beard, but it's gone. He's been to the barbers this morning for his annual clean shave – after all, for a man of his cultural identity, the word *terrorist* comes to mind more readily than *hipster*. It's time to get going. He pulls on his jacket, grabs his keys, and makes his way out of the house.

His mother is in the street chatting with their neighbour, dressed in her everyday widow's weeds, black as always, in perpetual mourning, but not only for her husband. He wishes she'd wear something with a bit of colour every now and then, but she's no different from any of her friends. She smiles at Hassan when she sees him, and walks across. The neighbour gives him a friendly wave and disappears into her house next door. It's a facsimile of his own house: squat, pockmarked, cell-like. "They'd both be proud of you," his mother says, and he embraces her. She pats his bare cheeks and smiles. "You should be going," she says. "There will be more checkpoints on the roads today. We will watch you on Channel 8."

His van is parked in an empty lot at the end of the lane. It's still hot even though it's late afternoon, so he takes off his jacket and hooks it across the back of the passenger seat. He winds down the window to let the stale air escape. When he turns the key in the ignition, the radio springs to life with more enthusiasm than the engine. As he pulls away, the newsreader is telling him three Palestinian villagers were shot by settlers this morning; they were rushed to the local hospital; it lacks the necessary equipment to treat their injuries; they're now awaiting permits to transfer to Israel; condition critical; they'd been working in their fields. In other news, water shortages are expected to... Hassan jabs at the radio, silences it. Not today.

Careful not to kick up dust or hit any children or animals that might dart from open doorways, he makes his way slowly down the narrow lanes of the refugee camp, a temporary township turned permanent. There were no cars to think about back in 1948 when his elders were ousted from their villages and had come here seeking refuge. He clears the dust from his windscreen just for it to resettle a few seconds later. This ever-present layer of ancient grit they're trying to get out from under. When he thinks of the future, it is without this; it is shiny and bright. Litter lines the front of the houses where flower pots should be, bringing some colour, still, to a blanched scene. He leaves Aida Camp via the main gate, passes under the twenty-foot concrete key that looms overhead, a giant replica of the real keys his mother, and plenty others of her generation, still keep with them in their pockets, symbolic of their right to return to their homes in that part of Palestine now called Israel. They really should demolish it, that ugly concrete reminder of faded dreams.

He drives through the neighbouring town, a larger version of the refugee camp: wider roads, taller buildings, heavier traffic, but just as dusty and littered. Wrecked vehicles, weeds and stray dogs share vacant lots between the shops and cafés, all family-owned and run, local because business with the outside world is restricted, but not too local because the Israelis restrict that as well, stifling manufacture, trade, the Palestinians' ability to be independent. And so, the shops are full of Israeli products, are lit by Israeli-supplied electricity, and their operations are taxed by the Israeli government. There's a reason it's sometimes called the "profitable occupation".

Hassan passes the shop where his wife works, a hardware store where they'd had their first adult conversation eighteen years ago, which had started about the relative merits of two different wood glues, but had ended with him asking her out. This afternoon, she's inside talking to a customer, looking as beautiful now as she did back then.

His neighbour is coming toward him in his beat-up taxi. It may once have been described as *stretched* but now it just looks *slumped*. Hassan smiles at the familiar sight, and they both come to a stop and wind down their windows.

"Finished for the day, Amir?"

Amir nods. "I've just brought some tourists from Jerusalem and dropped them off at Manger Square. They were generous with their tip, so I thought I'd take the family out for shawarmas. Why don't you bring Layla and the girls along, come and join us?"

Once upon a time, Hassan, Amir and their then girlfriends, now wives, were inseparable. They'd all grown up together in the refugee camp, gone to the same school, played together in the streets when they were kids, but the two boys had kicked up trouble in their teens and the girls had kept their distance for a while. Amir was the first boy to launch himself out of the back window that early morning back in '89 when Hassan had peeked through the living room curtains and found himself looking down the wrong end of a soldier's rifle. He's ribbed Amir for that ever since, even making a story out of it when he was best man at his wedding. They'd both had to clean up their act before they could snag their childhood pals. These days, they don't get together as often as they should.

"Wish we could join you, but I'm going to Israel this evening."

"That's today?" Amir says, a flicker of a frown darkening his features. "The big event you've been preparing for?"

"Yes, I'm on my way now."

"Well, good on you, my friend. I'll be thinking of you."

A car horn blasts, followed by another. They're holding up traffic. Hassan waves his neighbour of forty-seven years goodbye and pulls away. He grabs his phone from his jacket pocket and calls his wife. She picks up on the second ring and he swerves to avoid a pothole.

"I hope you're not chatting up that customer!"

She replies with a question. "Hassan, where are you?"

"Just leaving Bethlehem."

"How's your stomach now?"

"I've tried drinking milk to settle it, but it's not really working."

"Serves you right!" she says.

"I'm relieved the day has finally arrived, though, and I can get this over with."

"I could kill you for putting us through this again," she tells him. The ensuing silence says it all: they both know there are people out there who would relish the chance to do just that. "Oh god, just come back safe," she adds.

"I need to do this, you know that."

Silence again. The dog's not the only one who's heard it all before.

"I love you," Hassan says.

"I know." Layla makes it sound like an affliction she has to bear.

"Tell the girls I love them, too."

"Why don't you call me when you get there, you can tell them yourself."

"Okay, I'll do that. But in case I don't have signal..."

"Yes, then I'll tell them, Hassan. Don't worry. Take care of yourself over there, and come back safe."

"Always."

Hassan disconnects the call and throws his phone onto the passenger seat. They've grown up together as neighbours, so his wife has known both versions of him, the violent activist and the peaceful one. She would never have married the violent one, and she loves the peaceful one, he knows that, but he also knows she wishes he didn't have to be one or the other, that they had a normal life where it wasn't a choice that had to be made. That's what he's hoping for in their daughters' future, he tells her. She doesn't disagree with what he's trying to achieve; it's just that she worries about him. There are plenty of people in their community who do disagree with Hassan's form of activism: they think that by working with Israelis he's "normalising the Occupation", or worse, that he's "collaborating with the enemy". She's seen what happens to collaborators – the ultimate penalty is death at the hands of a lynch mob, and the very least you can expect is ostracism, your entire family shunned by the community.

He'll need to do something with the family this weekend. Amir's right, they should all get together, drive down to the Jordan Valley perhaps, take a picnic and have a float on the Dead Sea. But right now, he needs to focus because all eyes will be on him this evening.

He's come to the crossroads at the edge of town. If he turns left and joins the new multi-lane highway, he'll get to the Israeli border in under ten minutes, but that road is for Israelis only. It's one of the so-called "Apartheid Roads" built to serve the Israeli settlements that increasingly pockmark what's left of Palestine. No entry for Palestinians on those roads. He turns right to take the dirt road to the border and directs his thoughts back to his speech.

At that first meeting, I met Israelis who said they didn't want us all dead or cleansed from our land; and the Israelis learned that not all Palestinians are intent on driving them into the sea. But what could we do together, this unlikely bunch of Palestinians and Israelis, to take hold of that truth and make it grow?

Damn! There's a checkpoint up there.

The checkpoint is one of those temporary ones that can spring up wherever, whenever on the Palestinian roads, at best to bring inconvenience and intimidation to daily life, at worst, to maim and kill, depending on the mood of the soldiers. Hassan's getting uncomfortably hot in his shirt and tie. He stops at the checkpoint, takes off his tie and undoes his top button. There's a car in front of him with two soldiers talking to the driver through the open window, their hands resting at-the-ready on rifles. These soldiers are just kids, really, fresh out of school. Hassan looks at his watch, concerned the hold-up's going to make him late. If he were an Israeli, he'd be whizzing down the central lane of the Apartheid Road and across the border, halfway to Tel Aviv by now. The car in front drives off, cleared to pass, and Hassan edges his van forward and draws to a stop next to the two soldiers. One of them steps forward to peer inside the van. "What's in the back?" he asks.

"Nothing," Hassan replies. Anticipating such a conversation, he removed all his tools this morning and stored them at home. What would checkpoint guards have made of his chisels, drills, hammers and saws if they'd come across them? The result would have been confiscation, delay, most likely both. Layla won't be too pleased when she gets home to find the tools all stacked in the living room, but she'll understand.

The soldier swings his gun toward the back of the van. "Show me," he says, and then once he's finished his inspection, "Okay, go," and there's more swinging of the gun, this time in a forward direction. Hassan jumps behind the wheel and drives away as coolly but quickly as possible.

Another twenty minutes, and he's at the border crossing. It's a gap in a wall of grey concrete slabs fifty feet high, peppered on top with cameras and watch towers. This is the Separation Wall dividing the West Bank of Palestine from Israel. The Israelis began constructing it in 2002 and are continuing today. The excuse back then was that it was needed to keep Palestinian terrorists, notably suicide bombers, out of Israel during the period of the Second Intifada. But if you follow the Wall down its seven hundred-kilometre length, you'll see how it slices through the Palestinian towns, villages and fields, handing chunks of Palestine – people, sheep and all – to Israel, like cake on a plate. As long ago as 2003, the United Nations declared the Wall to be in violation of international law and demanded its removal. Fat chance. The Israelis have just kept building and land-grabbing. Back in Bethlehem, the locals have chosen to turn the Wall into their own weapon of resistance: a picture paints a thousand words, and that portion of the Wall has become a magnet for some very expressive street art. People the world over will recognise Banksy's murals – the white dove in a flak jacket with a sniper's crosshairs on his chest; the Israeli soldier holding a donkey at gunpoint while he inspects its identity papers; the hooded Palestinian lad throwing a bouquet of flowers.

Hassan parks his van beside the Wall at the border crossing, grabs his phone and tie and walks up to the checkpoint, manned by more child soldiers. There's a flow of Palestinians, mostly men but a few younger women, coming through from the Israeli side. They head to their parked cars or board buses, all making their way home from a day's work in Israel, back to their towns and villages. He's alone in going the other way. He hands his identity card and permit – single entry for today only – to a soldier who scrutinises the paperwork, pats him down and waves him on through a narrow, caged walkway. A thirty-foot walk and he's out the other side and into the twenty-first century. He boards a waiting minibus, empty and idling, air conditioning blasting. He takes a window seat halfway down and looks out on another world. Shiny cars pass him on the smooth tarmac road that's lined with palm trees so perfect they don't look real. As the bus pulls out of the car park, he notices a billboard showing a man smiling and swinging a golf club on a startling-green fairway, his two buddies behind him looking equally happy with life.

Hassan turns his attention to the stream of cold air blasting down on him from the overhead vent. He reaches up to shut it off and his stomach lurches with a sudden realisation: he's left his jacket hanging on the back of the passenger seat of his van. There's no going back for it now, that's for sure. Apart from the risk of being denied re-entry into Israel on the poxy permit he's got, he'll also be late for the event and he's the opening speaker. Everyone else will be in suits, all wanting to look their best tonight, but there's nothing he can do about it: he's let the side down already.

He tightens his tie and smooths the front of his shirt. It will have to do.

Fifty minutes later, the bus is making its way along Tel Aviv's sea front. Hassan gets out his phone and makes a video to show the family when he gets home later. Golden sand stretches down to the sea where waves break gently, a group of teenagers in bikinis and boardshorts are in the middle of the beach playing what he thinks must be volleyball, kiteboarders skim across waves close to the shore, while further out, sailing boats of all sizes dance a lazy minuet in front of a sun dipping to touch the horizon. The promenade is bustling with people out for an evening stroll, many walking their dogs, or sitting at outdoor cafés and bars, sipping drinks, talking, watching the world go by. There are art galleries, ice-cream parlours, souvenir shops. Everywhere, people are unhurried, relaxed. It's another world here in Tel Aviv. It's why they call it "the Bubble", everyone going happily about their lives with little thought or concern for what's going on just a few kilometres down the road on the other side of the Wall. Everything looks so much brighter and sharper here, free of the dust and grit that surrounds him at home.

Daylight is fading by the time the bus reaches the sports arena. The building in front of him looks like the alien spaceship out of *Close Encounters of a Third Kind*. The film terrified him when he was a kid, and what's in front of him now terrifies him even more. His hands are shaking as he checks his phone. Good, he's still got a signal. He calls home as he navigates his way through the packed car park toward the bright lights of the arena's main entrance. Layla answers and puts him on speaker.

"Hey, I'm here! I hope you're all watching on TV?"

"Yes, Daddy, we are," answers his eldest daughter. "The crowds are huge!" the younger one pipes in. "It's amazing. You're going to be famous!"

"Well, wish me luck, I'm going in..."

An excited chorus of "Good luck, Daddy", "Good luck, Hassan", "Good luck, son", comes back at him.

"Love you all."

He smiles and disconnects.

His daughter was right: the arena is packed. The vast floor area as well as the terraced seating is completely full. He'd been told to expect it, of course, with people keen to be there in person again after Covid lockdowns forced the event online for the last two years. The arena is open-air and the night is humid. Sweat breaks out on Hassan's brow. The stage at the front is huge, fit for a rock concert, with thirty-foot LED video walls on either side. He makes his way down the aisle on the far-left, as he's been directed, and finds the door to the backstage area. He knocks and the door immediately swings open, revealing two men dressed in black with anxious faces. "Mr. Hassan?" one of them asks hopefully, while the other speaks hurriedly into a walkie-talkie. Hassan nods. "Great. Cutting it a bit fine there, but you're here now. Please, this way." And Hassan is led up some steps to the side of the stage.

Eight o'clock, the lights dim across the arena, and a whispery quiet descends on the seated audience. A siren sounds, joined by tens of others across the city, a minute's silence in respect for the fallen. It stops, and into the hush the lights suddenly blare. Hassan's time has come. He steps onto the stage and walks slowly toward the centre. He's acutely aware of his limp, or, more accurately, he's acutely aware that everyone else is aware of his limp. A legacy from his childhood, the lack of a polio shot. Another man is coming from the opposite direction. The applause is thunderous. The lights are blinding. They meet in the middle, Hassan and this other man. Hassan thinks of his family huddled together in the living room back in Aida, watching this on television. Then he notices something about the other man: he's got rolled-up sleeves and a loosened tie. He's jacketless, too. Hassan grabs the man and pulls him toward him. Hugs him. Caleb. He's an Israeli, and is as close to Hassan as the brother he's lost.

2

Caleb

Present Day – Millennium Arena, Tel Aviv

Their welcome from the ten thousand people packing the arena is deafening. Twenty times that number are tuning in via web streaming, plus the local television networks are covering the event live. This is Caleb's first public appearance since the refusenik scandal and that disastrous television interview he did seventeen years ago. He quickens his pace toward Hassan and hugs him as if he were a life raft in a storm. Thank goodness Hassan is speaking first; it gives Caleb time to settle his nerves. They both turn to face their audience, and the crowd roars louder.

"Sixteen years ago, three Palestinians met with three Israelis in a hotel just outside Bethlehem," Hassan begins. Caleb knows his friend feels the strain at these events, always expected to open the proceedings but thereby taking on the burden of providing first impressions, of being the first face of the organisation people see. The pressure is on him to not look like trouble, and here he is, smartly turned out, confident, composed, a real natural and a hard act to follow.

Caleb tries to zone out, to retreat inside his head and calm himself by reciting the first few sentences of his own speech. *Memorial Day, a date on the Israeli calendar to remember our soldiers and civilians who have died in the bloody pursuit of forming and defending our State. So what right do Palestinians have to be here, you may ask, to be welcomed on stage like my friend Hassan, to sit in the audience like many of our colleagues, to participate jointly in this remembrance event, despite being the source of Israeli spilt blood? Well, let me tell you my story.*

And he'll relay to the audience how he'd been on the edge of mental breakdown when Hassan, this Palestinian with whom he's sharing the stage, saved him. And that it had all begun back in 2005, when Caleb was fresh out of school and conscripted into an elite combat unit of the Israeli Defence Force.

October 2005 – The Bravado of Teenage Soldiers

Caleb is in the back of a jeep, the lead vehicle in a convoy of five. He completed his basic training last week, and this is his first sortie deep inside Palestinian territory. He's nervous, but also curious to encounter the violent type of Palestinian he's expecting to find out here. Of course, he's come across Palestinians before. There are the Arab Israeli day labourers back home on his kibbutz – the Palestinians who remained on their land after Israel declared its state there in 1948. They keep to themselves, really, walking in from their village each morning, putting in a good day's work and leaving quietly at the end of their shift. Then there are the Palestinians who come and go from the Israeli settlements he was sent to guard during his basic training.

These settlements were just across the border into the West Bank, and their factories employed Palestinians from the surrounding area. The Palestinians would park their cars on the side of the roads leading to the settlements and file past security at the front gates by foot. It had been Caleb's job back then to man the gate, check the permits, make sure all comings and goings went smoothly, which they always tended to do. It was really boring work, actually. But now he's ready to do some real work, encounter the other Palestinians: the thugs out on the streets throwing rocks and petrol bombs at his fellow soldiers; the terrorists ready with their concealed explosives; the anarchists who want to drive all Israelis into the sea. These Palestinians are the enemy, and he's proud to be part of the *World's Most Moral Army*, doing his bit to defend Israel against them.

"We're diverting to Khaybar, one of the cave communities ten kilometres south of Hebron," says his unit commander from the front passenger seat, turning to address the six soldiers behind him. "There's reports of trouble between the cave dwellers and some of the residents of a nearby settlement."

Palestinians kicking up trouble! At last, some real action! Caleb looks at his comrades sat opposite him, three of them squashed side-by-side on a bench seat, and he sees the excitement flit across their faces, energise their bodies. Yes, they feel it too – the eagerness to get there, to pile out of the jeep in a show of force, to wield their guns and demonstrate their might, to crush the threat of Palestinian violence.

"Listen, lads," the commander continues, "we're deep inside the Occupied Territories now, where things get real. It's time to put all that training to good use. At best, these people don't want you here; most likely, they want you dead." Caleb sits taller, clenches his fists. The guys sitting opposite him can barely suppress grins. "They're illegals," says the commander, "still living out here in caves when they should be moving into the Area A towns. This is Area C – it's all Israeli territory now."

Ah yes! Caleb remembers this from high school last year when he'd researched the Oslo Accords for an essay. Area A: Palestinians only; the main towns; eighteen percent of Palestine's West Bank; under Palestinian Authority control. Area B: Palestinians only; scattered villages; twenty-two percent of the West Bank; under joint Israeli/Palestinian control. Nearly three million Palestinians live in Areas A and B. Area C: sixty percent of the West Bank; under Israeli control (for its settlements, security, expansion); Israelis only (390,000 of them at the last count, and growing rapidly) but 150,000 Palestinians still living there.

Caleb peers out the front of the jeep, trying to get a better look at their surroundings. It's just scrubland they're passing through: rubble and rocks, a scattering of emaciated-looking bushes. Why would anyone want to live out here? How do they even survive? The road they're driving on leads way into the distance and meanders up a hill to a town of some sort perched at the top. As they get closer, Caleb can make out more detail: rows of houses; modern, beige, ubiquitous. Electricity poles follow the length of the road, right up to the town. Unnaturally green grass cloaks the shoulders of the hill and willowy cypress trees and shocking pink bougainvillea screen a high brick wall at its neckline, encircling the town. Clearly, there's plenty of surplus water up there for irrigation. Behind the wall, a cluster of kites flutter high in the sky, bright, colourful, optimistic.

"Israeli colony," says the soldier next to him. "Or *settlement*, if you want the official word for it."

"Out this far?" Caleb is surprised: it's so isolated out here.

"Yes, of course. That's part of the great masterplan. If Israel can cover the whole of the West Bank with settlements, it's more difficult for the international community to force Israel to leave," the other soldier replies. This is Ethan, Caleb's assigned partner, unfortunately. "Occupation today, annexation tomorrow," Ethan continues. "The settlements are illegal under international law, but our government doesn't care about that. Illegal settlements serving an illegal occupation."

The three soldiers opposite roll their eyes and look away. He's Caleb's problem to deal with.

Their commander turns to them again. "The State has tried to move the cave dwellers into Area A towns over the last few years, to clear them out of here, but they refuse to go," he explains. "And now they've started building their own houses from rocks and mud. They knew they were illegal structures, but they still had the gall to complain when they were bulldozed flat. Now they're living back in their caves, refusing to leave. Settlers from the town up there have been taking matters into their own hands, putting dead animals down the Palestinians' well to contaminate their drinking water, blocking access to their fields, burning olive trees, that kind of mischief. We can expect some action today, so be ready."

Caleb glances at his partner to gauge his mood. The colour has drained from Ethan's face and he looks ready to throw up. Caleb's first sortie and he gets paired with this wimp! He'd got a read on the guy during supper last night. Although they'd gone through basic training together, they'd not really hung out before because Ethan kept himself to himself, one of the quiet ones. So when they'd got paired for today, Caleb had sat opposite him in the canteen to try to get to know him a little.

"Looking forward to tomorrow?" Caleb had asked. "I can't believe we're actually going to get out there at last."

"Nope, I'm not looking forward to it at all," Ethan had replied. He hadn't even looked up from his plate, but had just kept playing with his mashed potatoes, making a criss-cross pattern with his fork.

"How come? This is what we've all been waiting for, to start putting our training into practice."

"I'm a musician, not a soldier. I want to be playing the violin in the Jerusalem Symphony Orchestra, not here, wearing this disgusting uniform and expected to carry a rifle everywhere I go."

"But this is what you signed up for!" Caleb is shocked. "We all did, back when we were sixteen and put ourselves forward for selection."

"It was my father who put me forward. He was in this unit thirty years ago. I wasn't consulted."

"But you must be proud, now you're here? It's one of the most elite combat units in the army, anyone would be proud to be a part of it."

"You're right. Back when I was sixteen, I did feel good about it, I really did. I could see what it meant to my father, to the whole family: I was going to follow in his footsteps, do my bit. It was all great. But things have changed for me since then. I found out stuff that made me question the role of our army in Palestine. I tried to get out of conscription, apply for a waiver, but my family wouldn't support it, told me

I would bring shame on them, so here I am: counting down the days until they release me and I can get on with my life."

"But we're here to defend our country!" Caleb's annoyance was building by the minute. "What's so bad about that?"

"Is that *really* what we're here for? You know that what Israel is doing is unlawful, right? The Occupation, I mean. And the way the Palestinian people are treated, the daily brutality they suffer at the hands of the Israeli settlers and the army in their own land? It's sickening. I have Palestinian friends who have been shot at, beaten, rounded up and imprisoned for days at a time, for doing nothing other than being who they are."

"Rubbish! I don't believe you!" Caleb didn't consider himself to be the violent type, but he was ready to reach across the table, grab Ethan's plate and smash his pretty criss-cross potatoes in his face. "Who are these Palestinians? Where are they? How do you know them?"

"During the last couple of years of school, I got involved with a group called Theatre for Peace." Ethan was matter-of-fact, quite calm in the face of Caleb's aggressive questioning, resigned, it seemed, to dealing with just this kind of reaction. "They promote connection with Palestinians through music and drama. My best friend's parents are members and they used to take me along with them at the weekends. We got together with different Palestinian groups all over the West Bank. We'd perform for each other, and hang out together afterward. We got to know them, you know? Some of them are now my close friends."

The very idea of an Israeli ever having a Palestinian as a friend was ludicrous to Caleb. The latter were an entirely different kind of people, to be kept strictly at arm's length. Okay, some of them work in the Israeli fields and factories, but how can you tell which of them can be fully trusted? Among them are the anarchists and terrorists, who want all Israelis driven into the sea.

For Caleb, being here, wearing this uniform, defending his country, is a calling he's never questioned. He feels quite sorry for the guy for doubting the importance of their mission, like you'd feel sorry for someone who didn't have a religion to put their faith in. He hopes he won't need to depend on Ethan to watch his back today. Their conversation resulted in him having a restless night, and when he woke up this morning, it was with the shocking realisation that not everyone around you shares your world view, and that it's unsafe to assume otherwise.

They are starting to get jostled around in the back of the jeep. Caleb looks out the window and sees they've left the tarmac road and are now following a dirt track, bumpy and potholed, that's taking them around the hill where the settlement sits. These lower levels of the hill are stony scrubland. A few goats are grazing here, denied entry to the verdant grass on the higher slopes by a fence made of chicken wire.

"Things have come to a bit of a head today because the settlers are trying to gain entry to the caves to evict the Palestinians once and for all," their commander is saying. "It will be our job to calm things down and prevent any harm coming to the settlers. Follow my orders, that's all you have to do."

As the jeep rounds the base of the hill, there's signs of a rural community. No mains water or electricity here, that's for sure. There's a scruffy flock of sheep in the far corner of a scrubby, parched field, lumpy with stones. Blackened tree stumps stand in tortured rows in an adjoining field.

The convoy of jeeps comes to a stop and Caleb spots a group of children huddled on a rubbish heap. "Out, out, out," the commander yells at his charges. Caleb jumps down and turns toward the children. There's maybe ten or twelve of them, their ages ranging from toddlers to ten or eleven years old. They're wearing ragged dresses and shorts, the boys are shirtless, and they're all bare-footed. But their faces are clean – and full of fear. They're only about twenty paces away from Caleb, and he wants to reassure them, to tell them there's nothing to be frightened of. He takes a step toward them, but they scream and run off, heading toward the field where the sheep are clustered. Caleb is shocked: he loves kids and they love him back – at home, they come running toward him when they see him. Why are they running away from him? He looks down at himself, at his heavy steel-toed boots, the camouflage fatigues and swinging rifle. He looks like a fearsome brute, even if he does see himself as an ordinary eighteen-year-old. *Jeez*, he thinks, *I'd run away if I saw me coming, too.*

The commander orders two soldiers to follow the kids and keep them under guard. "The rest of you, this way!" he shouts, and starts running along the dusty track. As they round a large chalky outcrop, dark cave openings appear, cut into the hillside, maybe eight or nine of them, with a front yard of sorts in front, flat and dusty. People dressed in ragged clothes are darting around in all directions, like a colony of termites whose nest has been disturbed. These must be the residents of the caves, Caleb realises. Neater, cleaner-looking people, all men, are dashing into the caves and coming out with armfuls of stuff: clothing, pots and pans, flimsy mattresses, books, dumping it all into a huge pile as if building a fire. And these must be the settlers from the town above.

The cave residents are agitated, upset; they're shouting and screaming at the settlers. One of them, a woman, goes and grabs an armful of items from the growing pile and starts running toward a cave. She's prevented by one of the settlers, who grabs her arm and swings her forcefully to the ground. She's dropped all her things and she's scrabbling in the dirt, desperate to retrieve them, her tears mixing with the dust. This is disgusting. Caleb has never seen settlers act this way before, the destruction, the violence. How can they think this is okay? A teenager runs toward the fallen woman, goes to help her, but a settler grabs him off his feet and throws him roughly to the ground. Another teenager, no, a young man, bends and picks up a rock, draws back his arm, readies to throw the rock at the settler.

The commander points at the young man. "Shoot!" he yells, and Caleb sees he's directing the order at Ethan. Ethan turns and gapes at the commander. Caleb knows he's not going to shoot that rifle. The commander knows it too – in an instant he's redirecting his order at Caleb: "Your partner's wimped out. Now you! Shoot! The thug with the rock! Now! Now!" Caleb lifts his rifle and takes aim at the Palestinian who's frozen in mid-action. Their eyes lock. There's no hatred or anger in those eyes looking back at Caleb, just hurt, fear, like the guy's on the verge of crying. These are the kind of people Ethan was talking about last night, aren't they, the Palestinians who are simply trying to live their lives, the ones the Israelis menace and brutalise, the ones Caleb didn't want to believe existed. "Shoot!" the commander yells again. This is all wrong. Caleb pulls the trigger, but he aims down, hitting nobody. Yet, the young man holding the rock drops to his knees, eyes wide with shock. There's blood in his hair. Caleb can't understand it: he fired at the ground, at the man's feet, not at his head. The young man looks at Caleb as his eyes slowly close and he falls face down into the dirt.

Caleb lowers his rifle, doubles over and throws up.

And Omar needs to get to a hospital, urgently.

3

Omar

Present Day – Millennium Arena, Tel Aviv

Apparently, international megastars have appeared on that stage, flying in from all parts of the world to perform in front of fervent crowds. Omar can only imagine it; he's never attended a concert, and this is the first time he's been inside any kind of arena. It's normally used for sports, he's told – basketball and the like – and the flat part where he's sitting is the court. The rows of seating surrounding the court ascend steeply, up and up, to the open night skies. There are steps leading up to the stage on both sides. Omar's closer to the steps on the right, but to reach those he has to walk past Eva and the guys with the TV cameras. He doesn't want Eva trying to stop him, shouting out to him, causing a fuss, so he'll use the other steps instead, even though it means a longer walk and more rattling of his tattered nerves.

Hassan's up there, telling the audience about the very first meeting of Combatants United back in 2006. Caleb is by his side, waiting his turn to speak. Omar fixes him in his sights, searching for signs of the boy soldier who'd fired his rifle and left him for dead at Khaybar Caves, but from the way Caleb's shifting his weight from foot to foot, the clasped hands, the puckered face, he just seems jittery. Where's that swagger now? Omar imagined him to be a confident type in front of a crowd, relishing the spotlight, but instead the guy looks nervous, cowed by the audience.

Omar is feeling nervous, too: he also has to perform under the spotlight this evening, but unlike Caleb, whose speech is all part of the evening's program, what he has planned will come as a total surprise to everyone. He's traveling the route with his eyes, rehearsing what he's got to do: walk across to those steps over there, climb them, one-two-three-four-five-six, go across the stage, straight toward Hassan and Caleb. If everything goes according to plan, it will make the evening that extra bit special. People in Combatants United have been waiting a long time for him to show his hand, three years in fact, so he's determined to make it memorable.

December 2005 – Pride Before a Fall

Omar regains consciousness in a hospital bed twenty-three days after the incident at Khaybar Caves. He feels airy, like he's floating on a cloud, and he's surrounded by the sound of a thousand flapping hummingbirds. He opens his eyes a little and they sting against the light. He can see his mother's face. She's blurry, but he thinks she's smiling. He slips back into sleep.

He wakes again, and she's still there. This time there's a second person standing behind her. His sister. He struggles to think, to piece everything together. He'd been running around, trying to stop the settlers from ransacking the caves. What happened after that? Nothing. That's all he can remember. He tries to speak, but his jaws feel like they've been wired shut. He tries to turn his head, but it won't move. "Just rest," his mother says. "You've had a nasty injury, but you're going to be okay."

He must have fallen asleep again, because when he next blinks open his eyes, it's only his sister there. She smiles and steps toward him. "You're awake," she says. This time he's propped up, and he realises he's in a strange bed. He can feel his body now, the weight of it sinking into the mattress. The humming is still there, but it's receded into the background, grown quiet. "You were hit in the head," his sister says. "Shrapnel from a bullet. It ricocheted off the ground and hit you here." She circles an area on the side of her own face. "You're at the hospital in Hebron."

He's had two operations, his sister tells him: an emergency one when they first brought him in, to remove a blood clot from his brain, and a second operation a week later to repair the shrapnel damage to his cheekbone. It's his mother who later fills him in on what happened the day of the shooting. She tells him his friend Khaled had taken charge after the soldiers left, grabbing a towel to staunch the bleeding, getting him loaded onto the back of his truck and then rushing him to the hospital. "The rest of us were running around in a panic, but he managed to stay calm and do what was needed. He saved your life that day, Omar," his mother says.

"I owe you a million *thankyous*," Omar tells his friend when he comes to visit a few days later.

"It's no big deal," Khaled replies with a shrug. "You'd have done exactly the same for me."

"Of course," Omar says. "But even so, I will find a way to repay you one day. I promise."

Omar is soon moved from intensive care onto a general ward to continue his recovery. He's been told he should be ready for discharge around ten days from now, once his stitches are out and the doctors have done some final tests. After so many days spent confined to bed, first in a coma and then immobilised by all the lines connecting him to catheters, drips and monitors, he's relieved to get out of bed, to start moving around again, reclaiming his old self. He gets talking to the guy in the bed next to him and learns he's a policeman, recovering from a broken leg and fractured pelvis sustained when his car went off the side of a hill in Hebron. His partner, the driver, hadn't been so lucky and had died on impact. They'd been rushing to the scene of a traffic accident, responding to reports of schoolchildren run over by a reversing school bus. The policeman tells Omar about how he and his fellow officers maintain law and order in the Area A towns, "the only places where the Palestinian Authority still has control, thanks to the Oslo Accords," he adds. But what really catches Omar's attention about the job is the uniform and gun that comes with it. Okay, because of its Area C location, he won't be able to work in Khaybar, to defend his community from future attacks by the Israeli settlers and soldiers, but still, his own uniform and gun – that's going to give him some power. "This might be exactly what I'm looking for," Omar tells the policeman. "The thought of just going home when I get out of here, carrying on as if nothing has happened and waiting for the next attack, to be made a victim all over again – that's not something I'm prepared to do."

When he's discharged from hospital the following week with assurances that the only permanent damage is the star-shaped scar on his left cheek (which he thinks makes him look badass, but his mother says gives him a "lovely permanent smile"), he doesn't head back to Khaybar, but instead travels in the opposite direction, to Ramallah, and he signs up to the Palestinian Civil Police Force.

It's several weeks into his basic training before Omar gets some time off. A weekend's leave and he heads for home. He hasn't been back to the Caves since the day of the shooting, and the place he'd never spent a night away from in his twenty-four years of existence now feels strangely alien. It's his same family he's drinking tea with, and they're sitting on the same rug in the same cave, but now he sees it all through the eyes of an outsider. Maybe, from this point on, he always will. He looks at his mother, his father and sister, all so accepting of their simple, yet fragile, existence. He looks around their cherished home – it's just a dugout in the side of a hill, for chrissakes, so rough and primitive; and he feels suddenly frustrated by it all. "Thank you for the tea," he says, getting to his feet. "I'm going up to see Khaled."

"And Farah!" his mother shouts after him. "She'll be very pleased to see you."

Omar groans. "You need to put those ideas aside for a while, Mother," he says, coming back to kiss her on the cheek. "We're both headed in different directions, Farah and me. She wants to settle down, get married, have kids..."

"And what's wrong with that?" his mother says. "You didn't think it was such a bad idea before. Why should any of that change now?"

"It's not what's important to me at the moment, that's all. If I come home now, I'll feel like a loser, a victim who's just sitting around waiting for the bullies to come back and do it all over again. I'm sorry, but I can't do that. I've found myself a vocation – I've got some control over my life. Right now, that's more important than settling down."

His mother shakes her head and turns away. Omar can see she's upset, but there's nothing he can do to make her feel any better. "See you later," he says gently, and he leaves the cave.

Farah's been watching for him, that's obvious. She comes out of her family's cave as he approaches and gives him her most winning smile. "Hi Omar! Welcome home! How are you?" He has to admit, she's looking good. Her cute, peachy cheeks and dazzling white teeth are what he notices first because her face is one huge smile, and then he takes in the rest of her, as if seeing her for the first time in a woman's body. "Hi Farah," he says, fixing his focus on her feet. "Is Khaled around?"

"He's inside," she says, sounding hurt. "Go on in." She brushes past him and he turns to see her striding off toward the fields, no doubt in search of consolation amongst the goats. There's nothing he can do or say to make her feel any better, either. He goes on into the cave and finds Khaled sitting cross-legged on the floor, surrounded by open books and scribbling on a notepad.

"Hey, not disturbing you, am I?"

"Omar, you're here! Thank you! I can finally take a break." Khaled is smiling broadly as he gets to his feet and pulls Omar into a hug. "It's amazing to see you looking so well!" he tells Omar as they part. "A different man from the one I visited in the hospital a few weeks back."

"Thanks Khaled! Yep, the police force has been treating me well – lots of physical exercise, three cooked meals a day and no chores to do," Omar replies, grinning. He nods toward the open books on the rug. "What are you up to?"

"Studying," Khaled says. "I've got university entrance exams coming up. I've applied for a scholarship, so I need top marks in all subjects. It's really tough."

Omar looks around the cave. It's as basic as his own – scant furniture, rugs on the walls and floors for warmth and insulation, no appliances because there's no electricity. Once night falls, the only source of light is the oil lamps. "You'll do it, if that's want you want," he tells Khaled. "What are you hoping to study?"

"Law. I'm going to get myself the hell out of here and into a profession where I can live in the town and shout at the Israelis from a safe distance. I might even go abroad to work. Maybe to one of the Gulf States."

"You're looking for an exit out of here too, then?" Omar says. "I've no doubt you'll make it happen. I'm proud of you, pal. I was never cut out to be a lawyer – all these books, it's just not for me – but a policeman in Hebron, that's where my future is. You won't see me returning home any time soon."

Khaled frowns when he hears this.

"I know what you're thinking, and I'm sorry," Omar says. "I can't give her what she wants at the moment. Maybe some time in the future, once things have changed."

"I understand," says Khaled. "I guess it would be different if she was keen to move away, build a new life in a town, but we all know she wouldn't be happy doing that. You're right, it's best to leave her be."

As his weekend at Khaybar draws to a close, the relief Omar feels makes him unutterably sad. He can't imagine feeling entirely at home here, or anywhere for that matter, ever again. He's changed shape, incapable of fitting in anywhere. If only those Israelis had left them alone that day, if only that bullet hadn't done its damage, if only... He shakes off the melancholy and returns to Ramallah for his final stint of training.

Four weeks later, Omar is heading back to Khaybar, ready to celebrate with everyone. He had his passing out parade that morning, but nobody from his community had been able to attend. It's olive harvesting time, but it's not the picking that's kept everyone from getting away – it's the settlers up on the hill, who are doing their best to sabotage the harvest. A group of them marched down yesterday afternoon, wielding axes and threatening to cut down the trees. Everyone's on edge, fearful of what will happen next.

As he walks down the track toward the Caves, he's feeling proud for being the first in his community to have achieved anything like this. He's wearing his police uniform – blue and white camouflage fatigues, black combat boots – and he's feeling invincible, a returning hero ready to do his bit for his people. He passes an army jeep parked up by the side of the road and eyes the soldiers, lazing around on the ground looking bored, waiting for their orders. They watch Omar warily, but he knows they won't dare touch him, not while he's in uniform. Further up on the hillside, some residents from the settlement are sitting on the grass, watching out for the Palestinians to get back to their harvesting. When they see Omar walking along the track in the direction of Khaybar, they start talking among themselves and then one of them gets up and ambles down the hillside toward the soldiers. A minute later, Omar looks again and sees the settler heading back up to his pals, no doubt having been informed that Omar's uniform is Palestinian police – that he's just an off-duty policeman, alone and unarmed out here in Area C, and most likely visiting his family. Omar smiles to himself – his shield has held – and he walks on.

Everyone at the Caves has been waiting for him to arrive. Sure, he's congratulated by them all, told how smart he looks in his uniform, but it's apparent that mostly they've been waiting for him to arrive so he can accompany them to the olive grove. They believe the sight of him in uniform will be enough to keep the Israelis at bay until they've finished harvesting the olives.

In the tranquillity of dusk, the adults of the cave community make their way to the grove, leaving the kids behind "to look after the animals". They're carrying buckets, sticks and nets, their mission obvious, and the settlers' lookouts up on the hill spot them immediately and jump to their feet. Emboldened by having Omar at their side, the Palestinians enter the grove and start going about their work, laying the nets on the ground under the trees and starting to bash the branches, raining the olives down to the ground.

It's Omar who first sees them coming, a big band of settlers striding down the hill toward them. They're carrying torches, their flames glowing orange in the fading light, and when they reach the edge of the grove they form a line and stop, waiting a beat. And then they start throwing their torches like javelins, one after another, straight into the grove. After that, it's all a blur. The flames are taking hold in the trees, too high up for anything to be done, but still there's shouting "Quick, save them!" and "Fetch water!" and everyone's frantic, either swatting at the burning branches with their sticks and scarves, or running toward the well to get water. Omar sees Khaled and a couple of the other young men throwing rocks at the settlers, trying to scare them off, and the army jeep is racing toward them. The jeep comes to a stop and the soldiers jump down, rifles at the ready. Omar needs to calm things down, fast. The soldiers raise their weapons and shoot into the air, sending Khaled and his two friends dashing for a large rock to hide behind. A tear gas canister lands next to them and Khaled looks straight at Omar, appealing for help. The terror in his friend's eyes right at that instant will be forever seared on Omar's memory – because in the next moment, Khaled is running toward him and a soldier is raising his rifle and pulling the trigger, and Khaled, his best friend to whom he owes a million *thankyous*, has been shot dead.

4

Eva

Present Day – Millennium Arena, Tel Aviv

It's an immensely satisfying moment for Eva, a moment that's been two months plus sixteen years in the making: Combatants United delivering its message to a packed arena and, thanks to live streaming, the whole wide world beyond. She's been working with the production guys all day, helping them determine the best camera positions, testing the audio and lighting, running through the program, effectively keeping her jitters at bay, but now it's all underway she couldn't be happier with how the evening's going. Perhaps, now, she can relax a little.

As the Communications Officer of Combatants United, it has been a demanding couple of years for Eva. First they had the spectre of Trump's "deal of the century" and everything that came along with that (Netanyahu accelerating West Bank annexation plans; Israel's normalisation deals with the United Arab Emirates, Bahrain, Sudan and Morocco, Palestine's supposedly supportive allies) and then the COVID-19 pandemic hit, bringing a host of new challenges, including forcing this annual memorial event online for the past two years. It's been a challenge to stay positive and to keep moving forward, but tonight feels like it could be a turning point for them, a big step in the right direction.

She's standing with the production crew off to the side, and she scans the front row, taking in all the familiar faces, and feels a prickle of anxiety when she notices an empty seat. It's Heba's father who's missing and he's due on stage soon, right after Hassan and Caleb. She turns her focus to the back of the arena, hoping to spot him among the latecomers, perhaps waiting for a pause in Hassan's speech to take his seat, but no, she can't see him back there. She'd better go look for him.

Eva walks to the back of the arena, but failing to find Mohammed there, she heads for the exit in the hopes he might be outside having a smoke to calm his nerves before taking the stage. He's not there either. She digs out her phone and calls his number. It goes straight to voicemail. *Damn!* She prays he hasn't run into trouble at the border again. She makes her way through the car park, toward the security checkpoint they'd all funnelled through earlier – a fast lane for the Israeli majority, a much slower one for the few Palestinians. *There he is!* He's stuck at the turnstile talking to a guard. "It's okay, he's with me!" Eva shouts across, flashing her security pass. With a nod in Eva's direction, the guard hands Mohammed back his papers and stands aside to let him through. As Eva rushes over to greet him, she's startled to see what he's wearing on his head, faded but definitely scarlet. In an instant, her thoughts pass through recognition, to realisation, to gratitude. She places her hand on her chest and takes a shuddering breath. "Is that Heba's beret?" she asks.

November 1995 – A Time for Hope

The bus is already jam-packed when Eva and her friends get on. The five of them swarm around the driver, paying their fares in a buzz of teenage energy, before making their way down the aisle to find places to sit. Eva takes a seat next to a girl who looks to be eighteen or nineteen, a little older than Eva. The girl gives her a smile and shifts her bag onto her lap to make more room.

"Thanks," Eva says, returning the girl's smile.

"Are you and your friends going to the rally in Kings of Israel Square?" the girl asks.

"We are!" Eva replies. "It's a once-in-a-lifetime event! We're going to hang around the news vans, try and get ourselves on television."

"Cool! That'll certainly make a night for you all to remember," the girl says with an encouraging nod. She smiles then and looks away, bringing their exchange to a close. But Eva is intrigued. Despite her obvious youth, this girl has the look of a much older woman, of someone already worn down by life. Eva studies her out of the corner of her eye, taking in her shapeless beige T-shirt and drab knee-length skirt, her lack of makeup, the absence of rings or bracelets adorning her hands, just a cheap digital watch with a plastic strap.

"Are you from the West Bank?" Eva asks, turning to the girl. She's aware that a few of the Palestinians from there have work permits that let them come into Israel; they work as washroom attendants, stacking shelves in shops, that sort of thing.

"That's right," the girl says. "I live in Beit Sahour, but I work here in Tel Aviv, in a hotel down at the seafront."

"So, you're on your way home now?"

"No, I'm going to the rally as well," the girl says. "It all seems too good to be true; that we're going to have freedom in Palestine soon, that the Oslo Accords will finally bring an end to the Occupation – but I want to hear the Israeli Prime Minister say it, and I want to see Israelis celebrating it, and then I will let myself believe it."

"Wow! This really is a big deal for you!" Eva doesn't fully understand what the girl is talking about, but Eva likes her, she sees a fiery spirit beneath that plain exterior, and she's decided she wants them to be friends. "I'm Eva, by the way," she says, holding out her hand. "It's nice to meet you."

"Heba," the girl says, taking Eva's proffered hand. "Nice to meet you too."

"How did you end up working in a hotel here in Tel Aviv?" Eva says. "It's a long way to travel every day."

"I do it to help support my family. There's not enough work for everyone back home and money's tight. Luckily a friend of my father found me this job. Samuel – or *Uncle Sammy*, as I know him. He arranged my work permit, everything."

"Samuel – that's an Israeli name, isn't it?"

Heba nods. "It's a long story, and I know it's unusual, but our two families are very close. Uncle Sammy and my father first met about five years ago, when Uncle Sammy broke down on the road and my father, a mechanic, helped him out. They really hit it off during that first meeting, because after that, Uncle Sammy visited us on a regular basis. It was around the time of the intifada and he wanted to help us against the army – who were treating us extra badly back then. He'd bring his wife and kids, and his Israeli friends and their families, too, and they'd stay in our village during weekends. We'd organise all kinds of activities. Sometimes we all got together in the square and the kids played while the adults talked; other times we'd take part in joint demonstrations to stop the army from blocking our roads or imposing curfews on our village." She smiles as she reminisces. "We drove the soldiers crazy, but because we had Israelis with us they didn't dare do anything out of line."

Eva dives into her canvas satchel and pulls out a notebook and pen. "Do you mind if I write some of this down?" she asks. "It's all really interesting."

"Yes, sure." Heba smiles and watches as Eva flicks through her notebook to find a blank page, offering glimpses of loopy handwriting and brightly coloured sketches. "Are you some kind of writer?" she asks.

"No, I'm still at school," Eva replies. "This is just a journal. I write poetry and song lyrics, just for myself. Sometimes I scribble down interesting stories I hear or even just my thoughts, then I add illustrations. One day, I want to work in theatre, writing plays and musicals. After I've finished my army conscription and been to college, that is. What about you, what do you want to do with your life?"

"I'm getting married next year, that's what I want – to have my own family. I don't want to work in a hotel all my life!"

"Sure, of course not!" Eva feels she wants to say something else, to ask Heba why she isn't more ambitious for herself, but she has enough sense to know it's not her place to ask; she doesn't understand enough about Heba's situation. "Tell me about working at the hotel," she says instead. "I bet it's interesting, meeting tourists from all over the world?"

Heba turns thoughtful, pauses a moment before replying. "It's not really the guests I find interesting, it's more what they're doing here," she says.

"What do you mean?" Eva asks, nibbling the end of her pen.

"They spend most of their time visiting places in Palestine. Every day, they board coaches or get into taxis and drive across the border into the West Bank, where they visit all the famous sites: Manger Square and the Church of the Nativity in Bethlehem, Jesus' baptism site on the banks of the River Jordan, the Dead Sea where they have a mud bath and a float, all the while learning about the Samaritans, the Bedouins, Nablus, Jericho, Hebron, all these people and places..."

"To be fair, that does sound really interesting," Eva cuts in. "I'd love to see all that for myself!"

"Sure, but the thing is, the tourists don't seem to know they're going between two different places. Even Jerusalem's Old City, where they all stop off, is only partly in Israel. The question is, why do tourists stay in Israel when it's actually Palestine they've come to see?"

"I feel I should know the answer to that, but I'm sorry, I don't."

"There's no need to apologise, the answer's not an easy one," Heba says. She looks at Eva and, again, she pauses a moment before continuing. "You're young, but you seem like the type of person who'll take an interest in these issues. You won't want to remain silent."

Eva's not sure how to respond. She'd like to take Heba's comments as praise, but if she doesn't even know what the issues are, let alone have any answers, that just makes her naïve. "What do you think of the Palestinian Israelis?"

she asks Heba now, in hopes the question is a good one. "Are Palestinians in the West Bank jealous of their Israel nationality?"

Heba knows a few Palestinians who live in Israel and are its second-class citizens, those who refused to be driven out when the State of Israel was declared over nearly eighty percent of Palestinian territory back in 1948. "Pah! Not at all!" she replies. "A lot of them think they're better than us, because they stayed behind. But what life do they have here in Israel? They don't have access to the same education and healthcare as you, they can't own property like you, they can't get good jobs, they're treated as inferior. They have their own challenges, which are quite different from ours. They want an end to their inequality; we want an end to the Occupation."

Once again, Eva is stumped: she knows nothing about any of this and hasn't got a clue what to say. She's relieved to see they're nearing the Square and she busies herself with putting her journal and pen back in her satchel, then pulling out her lipstick and applying it deftly to her mouth. It's scarlet and worn to shock. She's been honing this look for a few months now: head-to-toe biker-chick black, studded collar around the neck, ring through the nose. A rebel. She just hasn't found her cause yet.

It seems that everyone is headed for the Square this evening, because the bus empties out when it comes to a stop. Eva steps down onto the packed pavement and looks around to regroup with her friends. She spots them a few feet away and gives them a wave. She turns to say goodbye to Heba, but one look at the girl's worried face and she knows she can't just leave her here. "Hey, would you like to join us?" she asks. "Please say 'yes'."

"Thanks, but you know…" Heba gives her T-shirt a dismissive tug and looks down at her skirt. "I'm not dressed properly. Plus, you're with your friends – you don't need any hangers-on."

"That's not true! They'd love to meet you! C'mon, come and say hello." Eva takes Heba by the arm and leads her across to join the others.

Whenever Eva has been to this square before, maybe to visit the book shop on the corner, or on some boring school trip to study the sculptures, the place has been near-deserted, but this evening it's absolutely packed. The City Hall at the far end is ablaze with spotlights, aimed at a temporary stage that's been erected across the front. A large crowd has already gathered there, waiting for the proceedings to get started. Behind them, toward the back of the Square, there's so much going on that the girls just stand and gape, trying to take it all in. Placards bearing messages of endorsement and of hope are everywhere: *Yes to Oslo! No More Killing! Two States for Two Peoples! Peace Now!* There are reporters talking to cameras, a guy playing a guitar, off-duty soldiers still in their uniforms, a class of schoolchildren gathered around their teacher, entire families, elderly people, young couples: everyone's here. A group of twelve or so youths, students maybe, are sitting in a circle on the ground amid the bustle, singing about how long some people must exist before they're allowed to be free, and how many times a man can turn his head and pretend not to see, and that the answers, my friend, are blowin' in the wind.

"This really *is* what Israelis want!" Heba says in amazement, so quietly Eva can only just make out her words. Eva smiles and puts an arm around Heba, giving her an affectionate squeeze. She wants the magic of this evening to go on and on, to take root and build into something lasting. And she's certain it will. Looking around, seeing all this excitement, feeling the expectation in the air – how could it be otherwise? Even a girl like Heba believes it!

The Prime Minister appears at the entrance of the City Hall and makes his way onto the stage. Flanked by four men in dark chinos and polo shirts, Yitzak Rabin cuts an impressive figure: broad-shouldered, impeccably dressed in a suit, shirt and tie, his grey hair smartly slicked back. When he steps up to the mic and lifts his hand in greeting, the response from the crowd is thunderous. Everyone's clapping and whooping – certainly there's no sign of dissent at this point. As the noise fades, Rabin starts to speak. He talks of a treaty at last, he says the Oslo Accords put them on a "solid path to peace", that they have already achieved so much – the mutual recognition of the State of Israel and the legitimacy of the Palestinian Authority – and recognition of an independent State of Palestine will surely follow; after nearly three decades of Occupation, security and peace for both sides will be achieved within months.

It's only now, while most of the audience is hushed, attentively listening to the Prime Minister's speech, that Eva becomes aware of shouts of "Traitor!" coming from the back of the Square. She turns around and stands on tiptoes, trying to get a glimpse of the hecklers. "I'm not sure what they're protesting about," she says to Heba, turning back. "Surely everybody wants this?"

"There will always be opposition," Heba replies, shrugging her shoulders. "But look at how much support there is for your Prime Minister. He's going to see Oslo through, I'm sure of it."

When Rabin has left the stage and, with a final wave, has disappeared around the side of the City Hall building, the stage lights dim, the cheers of the crowd ebb to a hum and the sound of John Lennon's voice fills the Square, *All we are saying...* People all around start to sing along to this anthem for peace; those who have them flick on their lighters and wave them against the darkening sky. The girls link arms and sway, singing along with everyone else. But then Eva hears the strains of a different anthem coming from the back of the Square. *Our hope is not yet lost...* It's only a few voices, but they're loud, jarring, punching through Lennon's words. *To be a free people in our land, the land of Zion and Jerusalem...* It's the Israeli national anthem, belted out as an angry chant.

Suddenly, an ear-splitting volley of firecrackers explodes, the noise bouncing off the high-rise buildings surrounding the Square and crashing back down around them. All singing stops and people are looking about, trying to figure out what they've just heard. "Fireworks?" Eva says, and the others shrug, shaking their heads in puzzlement. But then there's an eruption of panicked shouting coming from the front of the Square and people are starting to run. Eva is shoved backward and loses her balance, falling hard on the ground. Heba grabs her arm and yanks her up, pulling her back on her feet. They hang on to each other and look around. "C'mon, quick, follow the others," Eva says, pointing to her friends who are running toward the back of the Square.

"What do you think has happened?" one of the girls is anxiously asking as Eva and Heba reach them. "Was that gunfire we heard?"

Just at that moment, the urgent blast of a car horn sounds and they see a black Mercedes limousine pushing its way through the crowds of people in the road. It's inching toward them, headlights flashing, impatient to get through.

"That's the Prime Minister's car," Eva says, stepping out of its path. "Look, there's the Israeli flag on the roof and those are government plates." The girls try to get a look inside as the car edges past. The windows are tinted dark, but a camera flash momentarily lights up the car's interior and Eva thinks she can make out someone on the back seat, slumped against the door. "That's him – Rabin!" she says, recognising the suit and cropped hair. "They're sure in a hurry to get him out of here. What do you think's going on?" Eva looks around and spots a news reporter standing at the edge of the Square, talking animatedly into a camera. "I'm going over to see what's she's saying," she tells the others. "Anyone coming?"

As they approach the reporter, they catch some of her words, "...eyewitness accounts of a lone gunman... three shots... bundled into his waiting car..."

"She's saying Rabin's been shot," Eva says, spinning around to look at the others. "But how can that be?" Despite what her eyes have seen and ears have heard, Eva is convinced the reporter is wrong, that there must be some mistake.

"But who'd want to shoot him? That's just crazy," says one of the other girls, echoing Eva's thoughts.

Eva shakes her head. "I'm going up to the hospital to see for myself," she says. "Who's coming with me?"

"Not me," says one of the others. "My parents will be worried when they see this on the news. I'd better get home."

"Me too," says another. "And me," says the third. "C'mon, let's get out of here," says the fourth girl. They all turn to leave, but Heba doesn't move. "I'll come with you," she says.

"Okay, good." Eva nods. "Let's go."

The two girls make their way to the hospital, walking the three blocks in a tide of other people all with the same idea. When they reach the hospital, they find a large crowd gathering outside, anxiously waiting for news. There's been no official confirmation yet that Rabin has been shot, and if he has, whether his condition is serious. The air is buzzing with speculation and second-guessing as everyone waits, all eyes fixed on the hospital's main entrance – it's rumoured someone from government is coming out soon to give a statement. Ten minutes, twenty, thirty minutes go by, and finally three men emerge and stand at the top of the steps and survey the crowd. One of them stands forward, up to a mic that's been placed there. The Prime Minister has suffered two gunshot wounds in the abdomen and chest, he tells the crowd; the doctors have managed to stabilise his condition and they will provide an update in an hour.

"That sounds okay, doesn't it?" Heba says, turning to Eva for assurance. "At least he's still alive."

Eva gives a nod. "Yeah, let's hope he makes it," she says. "C'mon, let's go and get a hot drink from the café over there, warm ourselves up. We could be in for a long night."

Once they're seated on the kerb, steaming cups of coffee in hand, Heba asks the question that's on both their minds. "But what if he dies?" she says, turning to Eva. "What will happen to the Oslo process then?"

"I don't know," Eva replies. "I don't even know why anyone would want to shoot the Prime Minister when all he's trying to do is bring peace."

"But that's just it, not all Israelis want this settlement with Palestine. They're worried about their security, of losing their Zionist dream, of having to give too much back to the Palestinians, all kinds of things. I bet it was an Israeli who shot Rabin, one of those troublemakers we saw at the back of the Square."

In that moment, Eva doesn't know who to feel most annoyed with: Heba for suggesting it was an Israeli who shot Rabin, or herself for not understanding enough to refute it. She takes a sip of her coffee and looks at Heba. There's no point being annoyed with her, Eva realises; none of this is her fault. "You look frozen," she says, diving into her bag and pulling out a scarlet-coloured beret. She puts it on Heba's head and tugs it down over her ears. "There, it suits you – you can keep it, a present from me."

"Thank you, Eva! I love it!" Heba says, reaching up with her free hand to feel the soft felt.

"And look, whatever happens after tonight," Eva says, "I promise I'm going to understand all of this."

Just at that moment, the trio of government officials comes through the hospital doors again, this time accompanied by a doctor. Grim-faced, they form a line at the top of the steps and the same spokesman as before stands forward. The two girls look at each other anxiously. "It hasn't been an hour yet," Heba observes, and they both scramble to their feet to hear what he has to say.

"The government of Israel announces in consternation, in great sadness, and in deep sorrow..." The spokesman pauses, taking a deep breath before continuing, "the death of Prime Minister and Minister of Defence Yitzak Rabin, who was murdered by an assassin, tonight in Tel Aviv. Blessed be his memory."

5

Heba

Present Day – Millennium Arena, Tel Aviv

Heba was right: it was an Israeli who assassinated Rabin back in '95, an ultranationalist who opposed the Prime Minister's plans to make peace with the Palestinians. Eva had assumed it was a Palestinian who'd pulled the trigger, but what did she know about anything back then? She was just a naïve fifteen-year-old with a head full of silly ideas. She wishes her friend was here this evening, that she could show her the packed arena and tell her, "Look at where I am, at what I'm doing, and it's all because of you." She hopes Heba would think it's enough.

There are still extremists out there, people on both sides of the divide who are prepared to use violence in their opposition to peace, and Eva knows it's an event like this that lures them in. She looks up into the stands, scanning for banners carrying hostile messages, and then she turns to the back of the arena, looking again for signs of trouble. Returning her attention to the stage, she allows herself a smile: Hassan is talking about Combatants United's mission of bringing together ordinary Israelis with ordinary Palestinians, having them talk to each other, sharing their stories, getting to know one another. This takes away the *fear of the other*, he says; it helps people see that their "enemy" are ordinary people too, and once that's been seen, it can't be unseen. This is a movement that's gaining momentum and will surely end with peace, he says, and she remembers, suddenly, when Rabin had spoken of the Oslo Accords in the exact same terms that catastrophic night back in '95, and look what happened there, five minutes later, five hours later, five years later. Look what happened to Rabin! Look what happened to Heba! An icy shudder runs through her. *No*, she tells herself, *this is different!* But nonetheless, she finds herself scouring the audience one more time.

March 2003 – A Ballerina Doesn't Make Her Birthday

It's a labour of love that's been in the planning for days and has taken Heba all afternoon to execute: a Swan Lake birthday cake for her ballet-obsessed daughter. Amazing what you can do with a raw beetroot, shredded and squeezed, mixed with a bowl of sugar and a half-pint of milk from the backyard goat. The result? Pretty pink sugar icing to spread a lake as smooth as a mirror over a homemade sponge cake. Samuel brought a miniature ballerina from Tel Aviv last time he visited, and Heba positions the 5-inch pirouetting figure carefully on the setting glaze. Her final task is to pipe on the message, *Happy 7th Birthday Jamila*, but she'll need to mix up some fresh icing for that. She glances at the clock and sees it's just after four. Her mother left ages ago to pick up Jamila from school: they should have been home by now. She goes to the kitchen window and looks down the street, willing them both to appear around the corner, hand-in-hand and wrapped up in their usual chit-chat. She's telling herself to stay calm, that she'll see them any minute, but her heart is thudding anyway. It's always the same now, this dull sense of dread she cannot seem to shake, and who can blame her after last year?

She keeps the agony close, trapped tight in her heart and in her mind, because to release even a bit of it would be a step toward forgiveness, which is a no-go. The day it happened had started out like any other. The three men – her father, brother and husband – were the first to leave the house, headed for the workshop, followed soon after by Heba and Jamila for their walk to school, while Heba's mother started on the morning chores before everyone would be home for lunch. Midday came around, and her mother went to pick up Jamila from school, leaving Heba to finish the cooking and lay the table. She was back with Jamila before the men arrived, which was a little unusual, but Heba went ahead and gave Jamila her lunch while the two women waited.

"They're probably trying to get Suleiman's car finished," her mother suggested. "He needs it to get to Jericho tomorrow."

"You're probably right," Heba said. "That car spends as much time in the workshop as it does on the road nowadays – it should have made a one-way trip to the junkyard years ago." Her mother chuckled at that, and they both returned their attention to Jamila and the business of coaxing her into emptying her plate.

There was still no sign of the men when it was time to take Jamila back to school, so Heba packed up their lunch to drop off to them on her return. She was getting ready to admonish them – she had a whole spiel worked out about the importance of eating together as a family, that they should remember all the people missing from other kitchen tables when they decide to work through their lunch break – but when she arrived at the workshop, the place was deserted. The doors were wide open, but there was nobody around and her father's tow truck was gone. They could have been called out on a breakdown, she supposed, but why would all three of them need to go? It didn't make sense. Feeling even more worried by then, she left their lunch on the workshop bench and hurried home.

As she turned the corner into her street, she saw her father's truck parked outside their house, blocking the narrow road to all other traffic. She rushed in through the front door, ready to scold the three of them for being so late, for giving her the runaround, for blocking the road, but she was stopped in her tracks by the sight awaiting her in the middle of the kitchen: her father, Mohammed, seemingly returned to them as a ghost of his former self.

"Heba...," he said, turning toward her.

Heba shook her head, trying to clear her confusion. "Father, you're home!" she said, stepping forward to give him a hug. "We were getting a little worried about you. Where's Tariq and Mohammed Jr.? Are they upstairs getting themselves cleaned up?"

"Heba, sit down," her father replied, and it was only now that she noticed her mother sitting there, her head bowed, buried in her hands. "What's wrong?" Heba said, looking at her father for answers.

"Something terrible has happened," he replied. "To Tariq."

But that can't be true, was Heba's first thought. *Terrible things only happen to other people.*

Except it *was* true, something terrible *had* happened. The short version, the one she heard at the kitchen table, was that her husband was dead and her brother was missing. The full version, drip-fed to her over the days and weeks that followed, was no easier to digest. Tariq and Mohammed Jr. had been out on the main road between their village and Bethlehem, test-driving Samuel's vintage Sabra after they'd finished fitting it with a reconditioned engine that morning. The Israeli army had set up one of their random roadblocks, and they'd been forced to stop. Tariq was behind the wheel and Mohammed Jr. was in the passenger seat. The soldier on Tariq's side asked for their identity cards. "You're Palestinian," he'd said, on examining them. "What are you doing driving a car with Israeli plates?" Tariq had started to explain they were mechanics, that this was a customer's car, but then he went quiet, perhaps worried that he'd be getting Samuel into trouble by telling the soldiers he'd been visiting their village, giving them business. After all, since the start of the Second Intifada there'd been a warning sign at the entrance to their village, erected by the Israeli authorities, announcing in bold red letters: *This road leads to Area A under the Palestinian Authority. The entrance for Israeli citizens is forbidden, dangerous to your lives and is against the Israeli law.*

In the absence of an explanation from Tariq as to why they were driving an Israeli-registered vehicle, the soldiers ordered the two of them to get out. They'd resisted, telling the soldiers they were doing nothing wrong, they were on their way home, they should be allowed to pass. This was when Tariq had been hauled from behind the wheel and thrown facedown on the side of the road. He tried to get up, but the soldier standing over him aimed his rifle and fired. At such close range, he could have just aimed for the leg, but no, he'd shot Tariq in the back, right between the shoulder blades. Mohammed Jr. tried to go to his aid, but he got handcuffed and manhandled into the back of the army jeep. He shouted at the two soldiers, pleading with them to call an ambulance, but they responded by aiming their rifles at him and telling him to shut his mouth. So, Mohammed Jr. had watched, helpless, as Tariq tried to drag himself forward in the dirt, the blood slowly turning the shirt on his back red, until finally he'd fallen facedown and moved no more. From being stopped at the roadblock to drawing his last breath had taken fifteen minutes.

Meanwhile, when Tariq and Mohammed Jr. failed to return to the workshop, Heba's father had gone out on the road to find them. He expected to come across them broken down, but instead spotted Samuel's Sabra stopped at a checkpoint. If he'd got there earlier, he would have simply told the soldiers the truth – that the car wasn't stolen, it belonged to his friend, Samuel Cohen – and he'd have given them Samuel's details to check for themselves. It could all have ended so differently. But he was too late, and could only watch as the bloodied corpse of his son-in-law was manhandled into the back of a jeep and left facedown at the feet of his hysterical son before the doors were slammed shut and the soldiers drove them away.

Heba's father called Samuel that afternoon: he had to tell him to go and claim his car at the checkpoint before it got impounded by Israeli security services, but also, Samuel still had connections in the army and they needed his help to find out where they'd taken Mohammed Jr. and what they'd done with Tariq's body. Samuel tracked Mohammed Jr. down to a holding facility in Jerusalem. He was being held in *administrative detention*, and they all knew what that meant: no charges, no trial, just incarceration for an indeterminate length of time. In the end, it was for three weeks, and although Mohammed Jr. is home again now, he will never be the same. Their local clinic has diagnosed him with PTSD, but the staff are not sure how to treat him. As for Tariq, his body was delivered back to Heba via the Palestinian Authority a week after the shooting, without a word of explanation or apology from the Israeli government.

The girl at the Kings of Israel Square, so full of hope, is long gone. She's now twenty-six and a widow. But she's got her daughter, her beautiful Jamila. They'd wanted more children, two or even three more, but there's no chance of that now. Jamila is all she has left, and she deserves to feel very special tomorrow. Heba's got her the ballet costume she's been longing for – purple not pink – and complete with tutu and satin slippers. The musical jewellery box with the rotating ballerina is an extra surprise. It's all wrapped up and hidden under the bed. Jamila's going to be so excited when she opens it! And to make her day even more memorable, her teacher has said she can dance solo at the school assembly tomorrow.

Heba quickly clears up the telltale mess in the kitchen and hides the cake in a cupboard, away from prying eyes. She'll have to finish it this evening, once Jamila has gone to bed. She puts on her coat and leaves the house, hurrying toward the school at the other end of the village.

There have been more army patrols in the village recently, ever since the bulldozers arrived to dig foundations for the Wall. Understandably, the residents of Beit Sahour were extremely distressed when they saw its proposed route, hugging the ring road and effectively cutting off the village's fields, annexing them to Israel. Olive trees, vegetable patches, grazing for their sheep and goats, all gone. The villagers have been doing what they can to protest – blocking the road to construction vehicles by day, removing building materials at night – and now a military curfew has been imposed. Everyone must be back in their houses by five o'clock each evening and remain there until six o'clock the following morning.

Just last week, Heba's mother and daughter got escorted home by a soldier, marched down the street like a couple of prisoners. He'd deposited them at the front door and told Heba if it happened again, they'd be taken away for processing. "We were only talking to the construction workers," Jamila had said when asked what on earth they'd been doing. "We told them to hurry up and finish the Wall," her mother had added, "and then to stay on their side of it and to keep out of our country, like they promised us ten years ago." They'd both shrugged off her pleas to stay away in future and not get involved, and Heba knew then it was only a matter of time before they'd get themselves into trouble again. They've both been taken away this time, she's sure of it. Or, more likely, her mother's been taken away and Jamila has been left on the street, alone and distraught, to find her own way home. A shiver runs across Heba's back, down her arms. She wants to break into a run, but that would make her fears real. Instead, she walks.

"Heba, there you are! Jamila's been hit! Quick, follow me!" It's a neighbour calling to her, one of the other parents from school. *Hit? By who? One of the other kids? A car?* Heba starts to run, following her neighbour, and he's calling back at her, something about an army jeep, soldiers, a standoff.

She hopes they don't block her way; she needs to get to her daughter! She stumbles as her foot catches the edge of a pothole, and she curses and pushes herself up, running off the pain. She rounds the last corner and the school's in sight. There's an army jeep there, stopped in the middle of the road, and the soldiers are facing off against a crowd of parents and kids. Some of the teachers are there, too. They're shouting at the soldiers: "Call an ambulance!", "Take her in the jeep!", "There's too much blood!", but the soldiers are just standing there, expressions impassive and hands clasped around their rifles.

As Heba runs toward the school, she's calling out Jamila's name, over and over, as her feet slap the ground and her arms, pumping like pistons, propel her on, taking her the final thirty feet, twenty, ten, and when she gets there, the crowd falls quiet, parts to let her through. She doesn't want them to do that. She wants to yell at them to stop it, to ignore her, because everything is fine. She sees Jamila's school bag first, discarded in the road. *Why hasn't anyone picked that up? Fancy just leaving it there!* And then she sees Jamila. She's laid on her back, eyes closed. *Oh god, she's knocked herself out! She's tripped up, getting out of the way of the jeep, hit herself falling.* A folded sweater has been propped under her head; Heba numbly registers that it's soaked with blood. Two of the teachers are kneeling by Jamila's side, stroking her face, gently calling her name, urging her to wake up. Heba's mother is there too, sitting in the dirt with Jamila's hand clasped in her own. Her tear-stained face is a mask of agony, and she's making the most tortured keening sound, but still Heba's brain refuses to acknowledge what's happening. She grabs her mother's arm and starts shouting at her to get up out of the dirt, and then she falls to her knees and tries to lift Jamila into her arms. "Help me! Help me! I need to get her home," she cries out, as gentle hands push her back down and prise her away from her daughter.

The army ambulance draws up, khaki green, armoured and menacing, and stops at the edge of the crowd. Jamila is lifted onto a stretcher and put into the back of the ambulance. Heba is guided in after her, followed by her mother. One of the teachers places Jamila's school bag on the floor and the back doors are slammed shut. There's another person in there with them, a man wearing a white doctor's coat over an army uniform, and he tells them they're going to the main hospital in Jerusalem because they don't have the facilities to deal with head wounds like this in the West Bank. They stop once, when a soldier brusquely opens the back doors of the ambulance and peers inside. The checkpoint at the Separation Wall. They're on the move again and Heba registers they're now in Israel. She hasn't been here since she worked at the hotel in Tel Aviv, since before she got married, before all the bad stuff happened. She doesn't want Jamila to be here, at these people's mercy...

"They shot her."

Her mother is speaking so quietly, Heba has to ask her to say it again.

"I said, they shot her." Her mother taps her own head, marking the spot. "Right here, in the back."

"What do you mean? It's just a bad fall..."

"I saw it! The rifle, sticking out the back of the jeep," her mother sobs. "It all happened so fast. Some of the older boys were causing trouble at the Wall, shouting at the construction workers and throwing rocks at them. Then the jeep came skidding around the corner out of nowhere and a rifle appeared out the back, aiming at the boys, just as Jamila was running across the road. The rifle fired and Jamila fell down..."

The army medic has been listening to this, and jumps in quickly, assuring them that's not what happened, that their little girl was hit by a rock and they'll soon be at the hospital where they can treat her injuries.

When they reach the hospital, Jamila is rushed to the operating room for surgery to repair her shattered skull. The two women are led to a wooden bench in the corridor and told to wait. Three hours go by, without further word or comfort from anyone. Then Samuel arrives, rushing down the corridor, telling them he's just heard, and came as quick as he could. He goes to find a nurse, and they are taken to a recovery room to see Jamila.

Heba gets five minutes with her daughter, just enough time to kiss her and tell her how much she's loved, before the little girl gently slips away – and Heba has lost her final purpose for living.

6

Samuel

Present Day – Millennium Arena, Tel Aviv

"You decided to join us, then!" Samuel says, clasping his friend's arm as he takes his seat. "What took you so long? We were getting worried."

"I got held up at the border," Mohammed replies. "It seems your government has finally got wind of mine and Reuben's activities. They knew all about our visit to Jerusalem High School last week."

Samuel raises his eyebrows. "And?" he says. "What did you tell them?"

Mohammed shrugs, gives a wry smile. "I told them I was Reuben's driver, taking him to the school so he could give the kids a talk on architecture. They chose to believe me this time, but I'm not sure how much longer we'll get away with it."

Samuel nods. Everyone in Combatants United knows their access to Israeli classrooms, that golden opportunity to talk to the kids face-to-face, can't be relied on ad infinitum. They are constantly having to innovate, find new ways to reach the people. "Time for a change of tack," he continues, leaning in to his friend. "But more importantly," he says, giving him a nudge, "I see you're wearing Heba's beret! It looks good on you." Samuel recognises it as the one Eva had given Heba back in '95, the night Rabin was assassinated. Heba had worn it everywhere after that.

"I thought I'd wear it tonight as a *thank you* to Eva for everything she did for us. She needs to see we appreciated it all, despite what happened."

It's clear Eva believes she failed Heba: after all this time, she's still throwing herself into her work, whether searching for redress for what happened, or absolution for the part she played in it, Samuel isn't sure – it's probably both.

"That is a lovely gesture, my friend," he tells Mohammed. "Eva will be really touched."

March 2004 – The Problem with the Army Report

"It's been published," Samuel says. Mohammed will know what he's referring to: the army's report on Jamila's death following their internal investigation. They both suspect it's been a pointless exercise, that the report will be a complete whitewash, but nonetheless, they've had an anxious twelve months' wait for this. There's silence down the line before Mohammed speaks. "What does it say?" he asks, his tone wooden.

"It says what we all thought it would say," Samuel replies. "That Jamila was killed by a rock thrown by one of the local boys. It says he was aiming for the soldiers, but Jamila ran across the road and the rock hit her in the back of the head. Of course, the only witness accounts in the report are from the soldiers who were there. There's nothing from Jamila's grandmother or the other eyewitnesses on our side. Mohammed, it says the soldiers were doing nothing wrong, they were simply patrolling the Wall, keeping the troublemakers away from the construction site at school turn out time, and that they rushed to help Jamila when they saw she'd been injured."

"And no mention of Jamila's medical records from the hospital that have mysteriously gone missing, the ones that would confirm that bullet shrapnel and not rock fragments were removed from her head by the surgeons who operated on her," says Mohammed, finishing his friend's account with chilling accuracy. It's a conversation they've both been anticipating for several months now. Samuel was all for taking independent action much earlier, to not let his country's army get away with what they'd done, but Mohammed said to be patient and wait for the official report, then they'd see: there was no point putting Heba and the rest of his family through more distress if it wasn't necessary. So they'd waited, and while fearing the worst, they'd still hoped for the best.

"Do I have your permission to go ahead now?" Samuel asks.

"We have no choice," says Mohammed without hesitation. "My granddaughter was gunned down in the street just like her father, and now the coward who did it is hiding behind a state-sponsored conspiracy of lies. Jamila should have spent her seventh birthday dancing in her new ballerina outfit, but instead we buried her in it. Yes," he says, "we have to challenge that report."

"Okay, Mohammed. I'll contact my journalist friend straight away and get things moving."

"She's the one we spoke about? The one who interviewed you about the 'Wanted Eighteen'?"

"Yes, she works for Aaretz News, she wrote that piece last year about the failure of the Oslo Accords."

Mohammed's mood is lifted at the memory. "Yes, she was right when she said a herd of cows would have made a better job of things!"

"And she said a lot more besides," Samuel chuckles.

This is not what the Oslo Accords promised the Palestinians! she had written. *They promised them an end to the Occupation, the withdrawal of Israeli troops and settlers from the West Bank, an independent State of Palestine. Instead, the opposite has happened. More and more Israeli settlements have sprung up all across the West Bank, smothering every hilltop and spreading like a parasite across the land. The West Bank has been chopped up into pieces, each piece classified as an Area A, B or C, a system that's given Israel control of 60 percent of the land. The Palestinians' towns and villages have become increasingly fragmented by a web of Apartheid Roads and military no-go areas. The Israeli military presence has become more pervasive, more indiscriminate.*

And what about Israelis? What had the Accords promised us? Security. We saw it as a quid pro quo: the surrender back of land and increased economic freedoms for the Palestinians in return for security for Israel. Instead, we got the opposite: 73 Palestinian suicide bombings inside the borders of Israel, killing dozens of our citizens and prompting the Government to construct a 712-kilometre separation barrier to keep the "West Bank terrorists" out.

How did it all turn out so badly? Lack of goodwill, mutual distrust, feelings of enmity, tit-for-tat violence, the usual stuff. More specifically, we needed the newly recognised Palestinian Authority to keep the militant factions under control; to do that the Palestinian Authority started to build a domestic police force; we, seeing the increase of armaments being brought in to the Palestinian territories, suspected they were for use against us; and when the militant attacks continued, we accused the Palestinian Authority of doing too little to prevent them.

And here we are, a decade later and in the middle of a second, significantly more bloody, intifada.

"Yes, she doesn't mince her words," Samuel continues, "and this is just the sort of issue she lives and breathes for. If anyone can get the truth out, she can. Let's hand this over to her."

As soon as Samuel finishes his call with Mohammed, he gets hold of Eva to explain what's happened and to ask for her help.

"Are you kidding!" is Eva's response. "This story has got all the hallmarks of a cover up. Let's meet in the morning. You can give me a copy of the report and fill me in."

"I'll give you the statements from the eyewitnesses, too – Jamila's grandmother and the other villagers who were there and saw what happened. I helped them to prepare their statements at the time, knowing no one else would, and submitted them myself to the army. None of them are included in the official report, of course."

Eva gives an exasperated sigh. "Please let Jamila's family know I'll be doing my absolute best to get the truth of what happened that day out into the public domain. The army needs to be held accountable when it behaves this way; the Israeli people need to know what's being done in the Palestinian territories in the name of our *defence*."

Two weeks later, Samuel gets a call from Eva asking for a follow-up meeting: she's ready to discuss her findings – and next steps.

"It's as we thought," she says, settling down opposite Samuel at the coffee shop and pulling a file of papers from her satchel. "The army report is a complete fabrication, and I've got all the evidence we need to prove it," she says, pushing the file toward Samuel.

"Did you know I was an Observer in my army days?" she asks as Samuel opens the file.

"Aren't they the guys who stay back at camp and monitor the Palestinian towns and villages, watching for potential trouble?" he replies.

"That's right; the army has surveillance cameras everywhere. At the first sign of trouble, the Observer radios the nearest unit to have them go and check it out."

Samuel nods, prompting Eva to continue. "I had a hunch: the speed at which the army jeep appeared around the corner that day made me think it was responding to a report of trouble. I thought perhaps an Observer had alerted them, maybe seeing the boys in the side street next to the school and thinking they were up to no good."

"Clever thinking. I bet there's surveillance cameras all along that part of the Wall, where it's under construction."

"Yep! And I was right. I managed to track down the Observer who saw the boys congregating next to the school and called it in. She's finished her conscription now and is a student at Tel Aviv University."

"Great work," Samuel says. "What does she say happened?"

"Samuel, she witnessed the whole thing! She says the jeep came screeching around the corner right at the moment one of the schoolgirls was running across the road. Then she saw the girl fall to the ground and a rifle being quickly pulled back inside the jeep. She couldn't hear anything, of course, just see it all. But she's definite in what she witnessed. She told her commander, too, and wrote it up in her incident report. But guess what? The next day, her commander ordered her to change her report – he didn't want to have the army's investigation unit all over them. She did as he ordered, afraid of what would happen if she didn't. She changed her incident report to say the lads were throwing rocks, and one of them hit the schoolgirl in the back of the head. She's sickened by the whole thing, it's been taunting her all this time, and now that the official report's been issued and it's a complete whitewash, she's prepared to speak out."

"That's amazing, Eva. Are you sure she'll do it?"

"Yes, she's livid about what's happened. She's already gone to her lawyers and prepared a sworn statement. I have a copy," Eva says, nodding toward the file. "I managed to get hold of the medical report, too, with the help of a contact at the hospital. It says what we thought. It was bullet fragments the surgeon removed from the back of Jamila's head, not rock fragments. The soldiers who were there that day, and whose statements are the only ones included in the army's report, declined to meet with me. But that's okay – they would only repeat what's in the report, protecting their own backsides, and we have enough evidence now to completely discredit that report and to reveal the truth about what actually happened. Israelis might not be prepared to believe the Palestinian eyewitnesses, but they can't dispute records from an Israeli hospital. The official report was clearly a cover-up to protect the soldiers involved and the army in general. Here, I've written a full exposé," she says, reaching into her satchel and producing a sheaf of papers. "The question is, what do we do with it?"

"It's time we visited the family," says Samuel, "ask them how they want to proceed."

And so, two days later, Samuel and Eva knock on Mohammed's front door in the West Bank village of Beit Sahour. Mohammed answers, a muted smile affirming kindness beneath a worry-worn face. "Welcome, my friends, welcome!" He draws Samuel in to a hug before turning to Eva and taking her hand in both of his. "And you must be Eva. We are so grateful to you for helping us with this awful matter. Please come in, both of you. Heba is waiting in the living room."

Samuel has spent so much time in this house over the past fifteen years, and it has changed so very little, he feels the warm familiarity of home as he makes his way into the living room. He remembers the many nights he's bunked down on this floor with his wife and kids during their sleepover campaigns in the First Intifada. That time the soldiers came to the door and he'd answered wearing only his boxer shorts, and they'd been so shocked to find an Israeli there, they'd turned around and left without saying a word. That was the point, of course, why he and others came and stayed overnight in the village – to keep the soldiers in check. And over there on the table, there's the same old transistor radio, the one that Mohammed and he had sat glued to back in 2000, listening in as the Oslo Accords took their final breath.

"The Prime Minister of Israel, Ehud Barak, and the Chairman of the Palestinian Authority, Yasser Arafat, are being hosted by the President of the United States, Bill Clinton, at his country residence, Camp David. Seven years into a supposed five-year process, and the Oslo Accords have failed to deliver the final resolution and peace they promised. This is a last-ditch attempt to hold the process together and move it forward," the woman reading the news had said.

"Waste of those Nobel Peace prizes they were all given back in '94," Samuel had grumbled. "They should be made to return them, award them to a more deserving cause."

And then, as they'd sat listening, the next news bulletin had sounded the death knell.

"Within the last hour, the talks at Camp David have concluded without resolution, and with no confirmed plans for their resumption at any future date..."

"So, what now?" Mohammed had asked Samuel.

"A second intifada," he'd replied, "and I fear it won't be so peaceful this time around."

Unfortunately, he'd been right.

As Samuel walks into the living room now, he sees Heba sitting in the armchair next to the window. She gets up when she sees them and Samuel pulls her into a hug, kisses her forehead. She's lost more weight since he saw her a few weeks ago, and she has the grey pallor of the housebound. The loss of her husband, and then her daughter, are taking their toll.

"How are you, my dear?" he asks.

"Uncle Sammy, thank you so much for coming."

Eva, meanwhile, is rooted to the spot in the doorway. *Heba. Uncle Sammy. Beit Sahour. Surely not. Please, no!* is the chain of thoughts she later recounts to Samuel, but for now she just says, "Heba...?"

"Yes, that's right. You must be Eva, the journalist. It's a pleasure to meet you."

"Jamila was *your* daughter?"

They all look at Eva with concern.

"Yes," says Samuel. "This is Jamila's mother."

"But Heba, don't you remember me?" Eva continues. "We met at the Kings of Israel Square, the night Yitzak

Rabin was assassinated. We waited outside the hospital together."

Heba scrutinises Eva's face and gasps. "You gave me your beret!" she says, falling back into her chair. Eva dashes across the room and drops to her knees by her side. "Oh Heba! I've thought about you so often since that night. I tried to track you down afterward. I went to the hotel where you worked and they said you'd quit. Then I came to Beit Sahour and asked for you, but nobody would tell me where you lived. I tried, I really did."

"Why would you do that?" Heba is shaking her head. "Why?"

"I wanted to tell you that you were right, it was an Israeli who assassinated Rabin at the Square. That night, you saw the world so differently from me, and you knew so much more than me. I made you a promise. Do you remember? That I'd try to understand it all. From then on, I started to take notice, question things, try to see things through your eyes. Thanks to you, my army days were horrendous, the worst time of my life!" This earns a wry smile from Heba. "But it's also thanks to you that I became a journalist. I wanted to find you, to share that with you, but not like this..."

"It's okay, Eva. It brings me comfort to know something good came out of that night."

"I'm so, so sorry for everything that's happened to you: your husband, your daughter. I had no idea. But now we're going to do what we can to stop this from happening again, to other families."

Heba squeezes her hand but doesn't speak. Instead, she closes her eyes. Tears slide down her face and Mohammed leaves the room to fetch tissues. When he returns, Heba dabs her cheeks. "I'm fine," she says, straightening up in her chair and forcing a smile. "Please, sit down, everyone."

Eva settles into the armchair opposite Heba, while Mohammed and Samuel take the sofa. "As you know," Eva begins, "the reason Samuel and I are here today is to decide what to do, now we have proof of what happened to Jamila. The way I see it, we've got five options."

"Option one?" Mohammed asks.

"We go straight to print, get the story into the press."

"But then it's the army's word against ours," says Samuel. "They'll say the medical report is phoney, that the Observer is mistaken, and that the Palestinian witnesses would obviously point their fingers at the Israeli soldiers rather one of their own."

"Agreed," says Mohammed. "Next option?"

"We hand my exposé and all the supporting evidence to the Palestinian Authority. Ask them to pursue the issue with the Israeli government."

Heba sits up in her chair. "You're kidding. They've lost all their steam since the failure of Oslo. When's the last time we heard anything from the senior PA leadership? They're a waste of time."

"Option three is to go to a lawyer, find out about a civilian prosecution through the courts. But for that option, we'd need to know the identity of the soldier who fired the rifle. We can't prosecute all of them in the jeep that day. The Observer doesn't know which individual soldier it was, she didn't see the person's face, and the soldiers themselves all lied in their statements."

"Next...?" says Mohammed.

"Option four is to do nothing."

"Absolutely not!" Heba is outraged. "Let the bastards get away with it, for it to happen again, and again, and again? Jamila's death has to stand for something, some sort of turning point."

"Then that just leaves option five," Eva says. "We go to the army Chief of Staff, give him my exposé and all the supporting evidence and issue an ultimatum: retract the existing report and replace it with a full and accurate one, or else the exposé gets published. We lay it on thick about how it's so damning against the *World's Most Moral Army*, how outraged everyone will be when they hear about the shooting of an innocent child and the subsequent government-sponsored cover-up."

They all turn to Heba, waiting for her reaction. "That's the best option," she says after a pause, and the others nod in agreement.

"Okay, that's settled," says Samuel. "Eva and I will be heading to the Chief of Staff's office first thing in the morning."

The next morning at eight o'clock sharp, Samuel and Eva are waiting at the reception of the army headquarters in Tel Aviv. The receptionist looks bored with the day already. "Yes?" she enquires, looking from one to the other.

"We'd like a meeting with the Chief of Staff – it will only take five minutes but it's a matter of importance," Samuel says.

The receptionist is drumming her fingers on the table. "You'll have to give me more than that," she says.

Eva steps forward, hands the receptionist her business card. "It's regarding a report published by his office two weeks ago," she says, "about the death of a child in Beit Sahour."

The receptionist looks at the card. *Military Affairs Chief Correspondent, Aaretz News.* A key position in a leading newspaper, not to be easily ignored.

"Take a seat, I'll let his secretary know you're here," the receptionist says.

They go and sit on a hard wooden bench that Samuel immediately realises is not ideal for the long morning that lies ahead. After a couple of hours of watching other visitors come and go, they're still there, waiting. Samuel approaches the receptionist, who lifts her finger to him as if she's just remembered them and picks up the phone. "His secretary is coming through to talk to you, please take a seat for a moment." Soon enough, they hear the clack of heels coming down the hall and a woman in a smart black pencil skirt and white blouse approaches them. "The Chief of Staff has just left the office on urgent business, he's not expected back for the rest of the day," she says. "Do you wish me to give him a message?"

"Tell him, please, to read this," says Eva, abruptly getting to her feet and handing a thick envelope to the secretary. "We'll be back at eight o'clock tomorrow, and if the Chief of Staff is still too busy to meet with us, my paper will be publishing the contents of that envelope on the front page of its next edition." She waits a beat. "Beneath a banner headline. In bold type."

Eight o'clock the next morning, Samuel and Eva are directed back to the same wooden bench by the bored receptionist, and left to listen for the clack-clack of the secretary's heels as other visitors again come and go. Eventually they are rewarded, and shown through to the Chief of Staff's office by, it seems to Samuel, a child in army uniform. "Good morning," the secretary says, the tone of her greeting no less frosty than yesterday. "The Chief of Staff has a full calendar today and will not be able to meet with you. However, he has asked me to tell you he looked over the documents you left with him and he says...," she picks up a notepad from her desk and starts to read, "... in his words, 'Go ahead, publish your story. It's complete fabrication. The hospital says this medical report of yours is a fake – they have the original and it confirms that rock fragments were extracted from the girl's skull. The soldier who was the Observer on duty that day is no longer with the army, she was discharged on mental health grounds last year and is totally unreliable. And if the Palestinian witnesses continue to lie about this, they will come under our very close scrutiny. Besides, nobody is interested in a skirmish in some Palestinian village on the other side of the border,' end quote."

Eva is fuming. "It doesn't end here! Tell him that!" she says, turning on her heels and striding toward the exit. Samuel is angry too – this is his own country's army, shooting people and getting away with it. But what's left echoing in his ears is the Chief of Staff's threat: Heba's mother and the others who gave statements will be the ones to pay if they continue to force the issue.

Samuel and Eva return to Beit Sahour to give Heba and her father the news.

"The Chief of Staff is right," Eva says, after Samuel has explained everything. "Israelis don't want to hear these inconvenient truths – living with the status quo is simply too comfortable. But we'll go international instead, publish the exposé abroad, and put pressure on Europe and the United States to start coming down hard on Israel, to sanction the government for murdering innocent children. The world thinks this is a war between two equal sides, but the truth is that this is a brutal occupation where Palestinian deaths exceed Israeli deaths by a factor of eight."

"But if the article is published in other countries, we run the risk of adding to the casualties here," Heba says. "We're talking about the lives of my mother, our neighbours. No! We can't take that risk. We can't have more deaths."

"Heba, I hear you, but we also need to consider this: if we don't publish, we fail to act on our ultimatum, like we've simply given up and gone away. We'll look weak," says Eva.

"In whose eyes will we look weak?" Heba snaps. "Only that cowardly Chief of Staff who couldn't even face you when you went to his office." Heba has reached a decision. "Don't publish the article – it'll be our people, not yours, who'll suffer if you do. I will handle this in my own way."

7

Eva

Present Day – Millennium Arena, Tel Aviv

You can see from their body language that Samuel and Mohammed have been friends for a long time; it's in the way they lean into each other, how they incline their heads when they're chatting together. They're talking about Heba's beret now. Samuel is nodding at it, saying something, and Mohammed is reaching up to it, his face breaking into a rare smile as he replies. Eva feels humbled to see this. She hadn't even considered Mohammed would have kept the beret all this time, and the fact he has, and he's worn it here this evening, can mean only one thing: despite everything that's happened, he has valued the role Eva played in his daughter's life. It's a thoughtful gesture on his part and she must thank him for it, something she forgot to do earlier in the midst of her relief that she'd found him. But will this finally let her forgive herself for what happened to Heba? The questions still hound her: should she have tried harder to persuade Heba to let her publish the exposé about Jamila's killing? Would things have turned out better if she had? And even if she can find answers to these questions, what about all the other things from her past she still feels so wretched about? She'll never be able to wash all the blood from her hands, no matter how hard she tries or how much time passes, and that's fact.

On stage, Hassan is talking about what it's like to be living under the Occupation. He makes it sound dystopian, like it's not real and he's aiming for effect, but she knows from her own time in the army, and from her subsequent reporting days, he's actually spot on in his accuracy. It's funny, they've been colleagues for years, they treat each other as equals, and yet his current daily existence, his past suffering, is so much worse than her own. It's easy to forget that when they're so close. She's reminded yet again that the members of Combatants United are not all acting from the same place in their hearts. For the Palestinian members, the motivation is immediate and urgent: to end the Occupation, to stop the violence and oppression imposed on their daily lives. For the Israeli members, or for herself at least, participation is cathartic, a chance to atone.

September 2006 – An Intriguing Invitation

Eva is in the newsroom, typing up her latest report on army activity in the West Bank. It's all low-key stuff nowadays, nothing like the work she did on the army's cover-up of Jamila's killing a couple of years back, but it's the line she must toe now if she wants to get her stories past the editor and into print. Whatever that Chief of Staff had said to her boss, it had worked, because she's been under strict orders ever since to keep her material "tame". *Pointless, more like,* Eva thinks as she jabs away at the keyboard.

She's just wondering how to "tame" the fact that the army barged their way into another Jericho home last night, and took away another teenager for questioning, about more non-specified misdemeanours, when the phone on her desk rings. "Samuel Cohen for you," the receptionist says, immediately connecting the line.

"Samuel?" Eva says. "This is a surprise."

"Eva! It's been too long! How are you?"

"I'm doing okay, you know." Eva shrugs, reaches for her coffee, takes a sip.

"There was nothing more either of us could have done, you know that, right?" Samuel says into the silence.

"That's what everyone keeps telling me," Eva says, "but it doesn't help."

"Listen," Samuel says firmly. "I have something that will interest you."

Eva lets out a groan. "You know I can't run anything too meaty nowadays, don't you Samuel? Not since, you know..."

"I know, I know. But it's not a news story I've got for you. I want you to come to a meeting with me and another guy, Caleb Levy."

"*The* Caleb Levy who's been all over the news?" Eva says, her interest piqued.

"That's the guy," Samuel says, chuckling. "The meeting's next Sunday at the El Capitan Hotel."

Eva knows the hotel well – it's the big old one in Area C, over in the West Bank on the main road to Bethlehem. "First tell me, what's it about?" she asks.

"Peace," Samuel replies. "Three Palestinians want to meet to talk about non-violent activism. They know about us, about your journalism, my peace efforts, Caleb's recent protests, and they want to talk."

"And who are they, these Palestinians?" Eva says.

"I have to be honest with you, all of them have previously been active members of the resistance," Samuel replies. "Each one has taken up arms against us at some stage, but now they've renounced violence. They say they're using peace as their new weapon, and they've got a couple of ideas about how we can work together."

Eva sips her coffee while she thinks this over. "I'm not sure, Samuel," she says. "It sounds dodgy. What if it's some kind of set up?"

Samuel chuckles. "But what if it's not?"

He's right, she realises, this could be interesting – and exactly the chance she's been waiting for.

"It's been two years of treading water, Eva," Samuel says, reading her thoughts. "Knocking out those bland articles week after week that nobody pays any attention to."

Eva gasps in mock indignation. "Excuse me?"

"You know it's true. And I know you must be frustrated as hell by now and longing to do something more. Come on, you need to do this." He pauses. "Don't forget you told me everything, that day we were driving back from our last meeting with Mohammed and Heba. A conscience like yours nags for attention, it never leaves you alone."

Samuel's right again, on both counts: her conscience does nag, and yes, she had bared her soul to him that day, the poor guy. They'd been returning to Tel Aviv, Heba's refusal to let them publish the exposé burning a hole in her guts. She felt they'd both failed Heba, that they'd all failed her – the army, the government, the people, the whole of Israel. As if the loss of her husband hadn't been enough, Heba's daughter had also been shot and killed by an Israeli soldier and it had been covered up, swept under the carpet, and the finger of blame pointed back at Heba's own community, and there wasn't a thing Eva could do about it. "What do you suppose Heba meant by 'I will sort this out in my own way'?" she'd asked Samuel. "She seemed so angry. What do you think she's going to do?"

"I don't know," Samuel had replied, "but she's got her parents with her, and her friends there in the village. We need to take a step back, let them help her decide what to do now. We've done all we can."

They'd driven in silence after that, and then Samuel had brought up the subject of their army days. "Tell me," he'd said. "What was it like to be an Observer? That role didn't exist when I was in the army – we didn't have the technology."

"It was terrible. Absolutely vile," Eva had said. "I should have applied for an exemption from my conscription, like a lot of my school friends had, but it was 1998, the era of Oslo, and it was generally believed the army was part of the apparatus supporting a peaceful end to the Occupation. Holding that belief myself when I entered the army had only made the reality worse. After six months of basic training I got posted to a base in the West Bank, near Hebron. I'd been excited to go, like I'd hit the jackpot. This was my chance to do something positive.

"But I knew within the first hour of being there that peace wasn't on the army's agenda – and I had made a huge mistake. I'd got the whole low-down from my new roommate. She'd served nine months there already and was only too keen to rave about it. 'We're in the Wild West, we can do whatever we want with these people,' she'd gushed. 'Just last week, we rounded up some Palestinian kids who had their pockets stuffed with rocks. We took them to a holding pen, grilled them for their names, addresses, put the fear of god into them. When our commander cleared them for release, we decided to keep them a little longer, play with them. No one came to check. We stripped them down to their underwear, beat them, put cigarettes out on them, and they couldn't do anything. By the end, they were all crying and whining to be let go. We have all this power here. It's crazy.' She had this horrible manic grin the whole time she was telling me this.

"She told me another story, about the first time she'd been sent out on duty. There was trouble in one of the towns, and they rushed to get there. Their jeep was skidding out around corners, back door open, weapons at the ready, and as they got nearer they could hear gunfire, and their jeep was getting pelted with rocks being thrown from the rooftops. 'It was a real thrill,' she said. They stopped, close to where the gunfire was coming from, and could hear shouting and screaming. Palestinians were running up, down, across the street, in all directions. Their commander told them to grab their clubs and "get out there and take charge." They all jumped out, squatting low to avoid our own army's bullets, and made their way straight into the danger zone. She called it a 'real buzz'.

"I couldn't believe what she was telling me was all true. I thought she must be winding me up, playing games with me because I was new. But no. All this stuff was actually happening, and she was totally into it.

"The guys in the unit were even worse. They'd kick up every night in the dining hall, getting drunk on local beer, spewing lewd songs, pounding their fists on the tables, stomping their boots, cheering each other on. It was their way of getting through the experience, I suppose, letting off steam.

"I was relieved to be assigned an Observer role. I got to stay back at base and track activity in the surrounding Palestinian villages on a monitor in the observation room. Even that nearly destroyed me."

"How come?" Samuel had asked.

"Almost on a daily basis, I'd spot a group of Palestinian kids looking like they were up to no good. They'd be congregating on street corners, roaming the streets and gathering rocks, building roadblocks with tyres and any other junk they could lay their hands on to prevent our jeeps from coming through. I'd have to watch them closely, and make a judgment call on whether to sound the alarm. If it looked like they were going to cause trouble, I'd radio the nearest unit, guide them to the spot and the kids would get rounded up, handcuffed, blindfolded, and brought back to base.

"One particular day, I spotted a group of teenage boys on the monitor, five or six of them, walking side-by-side down the middle of the road. They were moving quickly, like they were on their way to somewhere, and they looked like they were carrying petrol bombs. I radioed the nearest unit and sent them to investigate. I was watching the boys make their way through the streets and giving directions to the responding unit. I could see the distance between the jeep and the boys closing, and then the jeep rounded the final corner and came face-to-face with them. The boys panicked when they saw the soldiers leaving the vehicle. They all turned and ran. The soldiers raised their rifles and chased them. One of the boys turned back and threw his bottle at the soldiers. They retaliated with gunfire and he fell to the ground. He was dead, and it was my fault – it was bottles of beer they'd been carrying, not petrol bombs. I'd made a bad call, and a boy died as a result."

Samuel had taken his eyes off the road to look at Eva at this point, pausing a moment before he responded. "But that wasn't your fault, you were just –"

"I know, I know," she'd said, cutting him off, "I was just doing my job. But that didn't make me feel any better. I couldn't stand to be there a moment longer after what happened to that poor boy and I got myself discharged as soon as I could. For several months after getting back to Tel Aviv, I was a complete mess. I'd go out to bars every night, get drunk, then spend all day in bed recovering before getting up and doing it all over again. I was living back at home with my parents, but didn't tell them what had happened, why I'd left the army early. And I didn't tell any of my friends, either. I felt ashamed, not only because of the part I'd played in the death of an innocent boy, but also because I'd failed to cope with army life while everyone around me seemed to find it so easy. So I kept it all to myself and I drank.

"It was my father who finally brought things to a head. He came into my room one day, sat at the end of my bed and reminded me that before I went into the army, I was planning to be a journalist. He reminded me how I'd come home after that first time I'd met Heba, on the night Rabin was assassinated, and how I'd told everyone I was going to dedicate my life to the peace efforts. 'I can't pretend to know what's going on with you now, Eva,' he said, 'but this is not the time to give up on life'. And that's when he told me he'd got me a job as a junior reporter working for his ex-army buddy's paper, starting the following week. That proved to be exactly what I needed. All the loathing and anger I'd bottled up inside – directed as much at myself as at the powers-that-be who'd got me into that state – would become my fuel. I'd find absolution through my work. This was 2000, and the Second Intifada was building momentum after the failure of Oslo. There was a lot to report. I started out covering low-key stories connected with the Occupation and I was attending demonstrations in my free time. My drinking had stopped and I'd started to care again. I went to tell Heba, but couldn't find her at the hotel where she'd worked or in her village. I wanted to tell her I was finally a rebel with a cause. And now I have found her, and there's nothing I can do to help her."

Sitting here now, in her office, sipping coffee, Eva realises Samuel's the one person who's heard her full story. Even today, those around her only know the bits she wants to tell them. *That must count for something*, she thinks, *plus I know I can trust his judgment...*

"Come on, what do you say?" he's asking down the phone. "Can I tell Caleb you'll come to the meeting? The spokesman for the Palestinians – *Hassan*, I think he's called – is waiting to hear from him."

"I'm willing to give it a try," Eva says. "Yeah, tell Caleb I'll be there."

8

Hassan

Present Day – Millennium Arena, Tel Aviv

Now that Hassan's eyes have adjusted to the bright lights, he can see the rows of people, line upon line of them, rolling out in front of him and rising up, all the way to the top of the arena. The roof has been retracted, and the sky is ink-black above. Out of the corner of his eye, he makes out movement in the far right corner of the very top row. There are people standing up there, leaning forward over the rails. One of them is waving the distinctive black and white flag of the defunct Irgun paramilitary organisation, the terrorist grandfather of Likud, one of Israel's present-day mainstream political parties. The flag's emblem still strikes terror in the hearts of all Palestinians – a rifle clenched across an engorged map of Israel that has swallowed up the whole of Palestine and Jordan, a symbol of Zionist aspiration from a bygone era that's shocking to see still being flaunted today. Other protesters up there are waving placards, and if Hassan squints he can just make out what some of them say: *No Talking Peace With Terrorists*; *Annexation Now*; *Hang The Traitors*. From the way they're all swaying in sync, it looks like they're chanting or singing, too. There's a television crew up there, catching a birds-eye view of the ceremony, and Hassan hopes they're keeping their cameras aimed well away from the protesters – he doesn't want to give his family watching at home any more reason to worry.

He brings his attention back to the main body of the audience in front of him, determined not to get distracted from the job at hand, and continues the story of why he'd become a local resistance leader, back during the First Intifada when he was barely a teenager.

October 1989 – Creating a Freedom Fighter

Hassan's father has just got home from his latest trip to the USA. He's been gone six weeks this time, a long trip, but it must have been worth it because he's brought back gifts for the family: a bottle of Chanel perfume for their mother, Hershey's chocolate for their grandmother, and football jerseys for Hassan and his younger brother, Karim. Their father sells products made from the olive trees surrounding the refugee camp: wooden plates and bowls, olive oil and paste, hand soap. He set up the cooperative with his neighbours several years ago, trading their wares to tourists from a small shop in Bethlehem, and it had gone really well until the intifada started and the tourists had stopped coming. That's when they decided to take their wares on the road, go overseas to find their customers. Hassan's father says this latest trip to the USA was his best yet, the carved nativity sets he was selling being a real winner.

Not only has his father come home bearing gifts, but he's also agreed to take Hassan's grandmother on a long-promised trip, back to her old village in present-day

Israel she hasn't been to since 1948. It's called the Nakba, the Catastrophe: the time when his grandmother, like three-quarters of a million other Palestinians, was forced to leave her home, her entire home*land* in fact, to make way for the newly declared State of Israel. That was when she and her family first came to the refugee camp. They'd expected it to be temporary, yet here they still are, suspended in this in-between world. At least at first they'd been left in peace, they'd had their independence, but that all ended in '67 with the Six Day War, when the West Bank was placed under Israeli military occupation. That, too, was supposed to be temporary.

There's an air of eagerness in the house as Hassan's parents and grandmother pack up the car for their road trip. The senior family members are excited to be going, while Hassan and his brother are equally excited to be staying: this is their first experience of being left home alone. The thrill of having the house all to themselves, though, proves very short lived. In the early hours of the first night, a loud thud on the front door precedes the sound of it being kicked in. By the time Hassan is out of bed and peeking around the bedroom door, a half-dozen Israeli soldiers in full combat gear are streaming down the hallway, bashing open the kitchen and living room doors, shouting for Hassan's father to come out.

The two boys are dragged from their bedroom and taken to the living room where they're made to stand, near-naked and shaking, in front of the army commander. Hassan has seen him plenty of times before, driving through the refugee camp, barking at his men and getting them scurrying all over the place. The residents of Aida know him as *Ice*, mainly due to his wispy white hair and pale blue eyes, but also because of his reputation. By all accounts, cold brutality is no stranger to this man. He orders his men to tie the boys' hands behind their backs and then they're pushed down onto their knees in front of him.

"Where's your father?" he demands, prodding the end of his rifle under Hassan's chin, forcing him to look up into those cold eyes. Hassan can hear the thud of heavy boots overhead, crossing the floor of his parents' bedroom, and then the sound of crashing furniture. In the kitchen, cupboards are being slammed open, their contents smashed onto the floor, drawers are being pulled out and upturned, their contents, too, strewn across the tiles. Two soldiers come barging into the living room; one of them starts slashing at the sofa, ripping the fabric and pulling out the stuffing, while the other goes over to the sideboard and yanks open the cupboards and drawers, emptying their contents onto the floor. Hassan starts to speak, to protest, but Ice shifts the position of his rifle, applying pressure on his windpipe and making him gag. "I said, where's your father?"

"He's not here!" Karim splutters. "They're all away. We're the only ones here."

Ice lets out a heavy sigh as he looks from one boy to the other. He shifts his rifle, aiming it at Karim's head.

"Is that a fact?" he says. "Then you two will have to help me instead, won't you? I need you to tell me where your father has hidden the weapons."

"Weapons?" The surprise in Hassan's voice is unmistakable. The idea of his father keeping weapons is absurd. "There aren't any," he says.

Ice nudges the end of his rifle against Karim's forehead as he looks at the older boy. "Want to try answering that again?" he says.

"Okay, okay," Hassan quickly replies. "They're in the back of his car – he took them all with him."

"Took them where?"

"To Israel."

"Israel?" Ice, the captain of cool, is suddenly feeling the heat. He lowers his gun. "Why the fuck has he gone to Israel?" he barks at Hassan.

"To visit his mother's old village," Hassan says, and Ice curses under his breath, strides to the door. "Anything?" he shouts down the hall.

"Nothing up here," comes a reply. "Nothing out here, either," comes another.

"Okay, we have to get going – now!" Ice yells, and then they're all gone, back out into the street. The brothers remain where they are, too frightened to move, until the sound of the departing jeep has faded into the distance, then they quickly manoeuvre themselves so they're back-to-back and with fumbling hands, manage to untie each other's wrists.

The whole ordeal has lasted no more than ten minutes, but to Hassan it has felt like hours. The fear is still with him as he leaves Karim in the living room to go and inspect the rest of the house: he needs to see if it's as bad as he fears. It's all wrecked – every cupboard and drawer has been upturned and had its contents strewn across the floor, every mattress has been slashed open, its guts pulled out. Even the pictures hanging in the hallway have been smashed from their frames and slashed to ribbons. His parents are going to kill him when they get home, he should have prevented the soldiers from getting in, stopped them from ransacking the house like this. But then he realises he's got a much bigger problem: by daybreak, the entire Israeli army will be on the lookout for a car matching his parent's brown Opel, every soldier armed and ready to foil these suspected terrorists from deploying their weapons on the innocent masses. Thanks to him and his stupid mouth, his parents and grandmother have become Israel's most-wanted criminals, to be hunted down and captured, dead or alive, and he's got absolutely no way of warning them.

Two agonising days later, his parents and grandmother still haven't returned. They should have been back by yesterday evening at the very latest. The two boys had kept themselves busy on the first day after the raid, getting the house back into some sort of order with the help of their neighbours. But today they've been left with only their thoughts to occupy them, and Hassan is terrified. He's convinced they're never going to see their elders again, that they're orphans, and it's all his fault for not braving it out and telling Ice there weren't any weapons. Why the hell did he say his father was driving around Israel with them in the trunk of his car? But the guy had his gun pointed at his brother's head and was close to blowing his brains out. What choice did he have? If he got the chance to live that moment again, what could he have said to avoid anyone getting hurt? These same questions, going round and round in his head, are torturing him.

"It's them!" Karim charges through the front door, grabs Hassan by the arm and starts tugging him to come outside. "Come on! They're home!"

Hassan rushes out to the street, where sure enough his father's Opel is making its way slowly down the narrow road toward their house. There's only two people inside. Who's missing? His father's there at the wheel, and that's his grandmother next to him. Where's his mother? This isn't good! But his father's smiling now, giving them a wave, so that means everything's okay, doesn't it? His father pulls to a stop and winds down his window.

"Where's Mother?" Hassan asks.

"Oh, we lost her in Israel," his father says, his smile suddenly fading.

"What?" Hassan yells.

"I'm just joking, Hassan, calm down. I dropped her off at the store to get some provisions for a special meal tonight."

"But we thought you were all dead!" Hassan yells. "You were supposed to be back yesterday!" He's managed to hold it together for the last sixty hours, to act the part of the older brother and take the lead, but now, at the sight of his father's unharmed, very concerned face, he melts into a sobbing mess. "I'm so sorry," he splutters, "I couldn't stop them. They came looking for weapons. They turned the house upside down! They threatened to shoot us!" His father jumps out of the car and goes to hug him, but Hassan bats him away. "Don't! I'm okay." He swipes the tears off his face as his relief gets quickly replaced by anger. *I'm going to get that bastard!* he vows to himself. Forget going to school, forget playing soccer or watching television – from this point on, Hassan's got something far more important to do with his time.

His mother cooks up a feast for the family that night: her special upside-down dish of baked lamb, vegetables and rice along with onion-and-feta bread, Hassan's favourites, and honey cake for dessert. This is what she does when things go wrong: she cooks. It seems the seniors have had nearly as miserable time away as the boys have had at home. Over dinner, their father reports that when they reached the location of their grandmother's village, there was nothing there. Literally nothing, not even any ruins.

"Are you sure you were in the right place?" This is Hassan's great-uncle, come to join them for dinner to hear about the trip.

"Of course it was the right place!" his grandmother shoots back. "Remember the three mounds on top of the hill we used to climb up to, to sit and watch over the goats? They're still there, exactly as they were."

"Well, I can't say I'm surprised," Hassan's great-uncle replies sadly. "The Israelis demolished all the villages as soon as we left, didn't they? It's what they did to make sure we could never return. I don't know why you were so keen to go back there after all this time."

"You know why!" his grandmother snaps. "To place the memorial plaque for Father and the other men who stayed behind. I don't know why you're being like this!"

Hassan looks over at Karim and raises his eyebrows: here we go again. This is why their great-uncle lives down the road from them and not under the same roof – the sibling fireworks that go off every time these two get together. "Uncle," Hassan says in an attempt to move the conversation along, "tell us the story again, about how you lost your leg. You went back to the village to check on your father…"

"That's right," his great-uncle replies, rallying himself from his sister's harsh words. "When we knew the Israeli army was coming, most of us left the village and hid in the hills. We planned to wait until the soldiers had passed through and then return home. Our father and two other men volunteered to stay close by the village to keep a lookout. They said they'd come and get us when it was safe to return, but two days went by and we heard nothing, so I set off with one of the other lads to see what was happening.

As soon as we got near the village, we came under fire. The bastards shot me in the leg! I don't know how, but we managed to get away and hide ourselves among the rocks. We stayed there for hours, waiting for it to get dark so we could make a run for it. We were able to stop the bleeding from the bullet wound using a scarf as a tourniquet, but it was agony. When night eventually arrived, we made our way back to the hiding place in the hills."

"We all had to decide what to do at that stage," Hassan's grandmother says, picking up the story. "We couldn't go back to the village, and we couldn't stay in the hills, so we made the hard decision to leave, heading east toward Jordan where we'd heard they were setting up refugee camps. We were walking for days."

"And by the time we got here, my leg was gangrenous and had to be amputated."

"We thought we were going to lose you along with your leg," Hassan's grandmother says, smiling at her brother with restored affection. "We never found out what happened to Father and the others," she continues. "Whether they were killed in the village, or taken away as prisoners, we don't know. We never saw any of them again."

A few days later, Hassan's father sets off for his next work trip and life is expected to go on as normal, but Hassan's fury with Ice is still smouldering. The way the rest of his family have put it all behind them, are moving on with their lives as if nothing ever happened, just enrages him more. *How can things just go back to normal?* It's impossible. A desperate need for revenge settles on him. Day and night, it's there, inside his head. He talks his pals into becoming freedom fighters, to take a stand against Ice and his men and drive them out of Aida Camp once and for all. And so, armed only with slingshots, knives and bags of bravado, they ready themselves to take on the Israeli army.

Not long into their campaign, Hassan and three other members of his gang are busy slashing an army jeep's tyres while its soldiers are off terrorizing the occupants of a nearby house, when another jeep comes careening around the corner, taking them all by surprise, and the four teens get hauled off to a detention centre, hung by their arms from the rafters and beaten with clubs. Hassan knows it's the army's unofficial protocol to "break arms and legs" and he feels luck is on his side when he and his pals are released five days later, bruised and battered, but with all limbs intact.

Back on the streets, Hassan and his fellow rebels spot Ice out on patrol one day. They sling rocks at his passing convoy and scarper, but unfortunately Amir is too slow and gets caught and carted back to the detention centre. He collapses under "questioning" and divulges the names and addresses of his accomplices. Hassan and the others are all swiftly rounded up and told they're "not going to be let off lightly this time". They're brought before the military court where an army officer acts as judge and jury and sentences each of them to three months' military detention.

Released and on the streets again, Hassan and his gang are undeterred. But by now, they're all on Ice's most-wanted list and he's on the lookout for them, ready to make their lives hell. They learn to live like fugitives, keeping out of sight during the day, moving on to a different place each night, never sleeping in their own beds. Hassan's mother doesn't see him from one week to the next, and she's been told three times already that he's dead.

It's around this time that Hassan first meets Heba. One night, he and a couple others from the gang spend the night in Beit Sahour, sleeping on mattresses laid out on the living room floor of one of their supporters. Hassan is the first one to wake in the morning. It's that quiet pre-dawn time, just before the cockerels and thrushes start up their incessant din. He goes to the window, peeks through the curtains and is startled by the most hair-raising sight of his young life. Standing there as still as a sculpture, rifle aimed straight at Hassan's head, is Ice.

Without moving an inch, Hassan hisses his pals awake and tells them to make a run for it out the back window. As soon as he's sure they're all out, he turns and makes his own dash for it across the living room and launches himself through the back window. He lands heavily on the ground below, dislocating his shoulder in the process, and he cradles his detached arm as he makes his escape. Sensing Ice closing in, he dashes down a side alley and nearly crashes into Heba, who's out delivering milk. She recognises him as a boy from the neighbouring refugee camp, the one with the limp from polio, and silently beckons for him to follow her. She leads him to her father's workshop at the top of the village, serving these days as a cow barn, and tells him to hide in the hay while she runs to get help.

From that day on, the Beit Sahour dairy becomes one of Hassan's regular night-time spots.

9

Heba

Present Day – Millennium Arena, Tel Aviv

Those protesters up there waving their flags and banners are all Israeli, of course. Hassan knows there are no Palestinian voices of dissent here this evening – the few Palestinians in the audience are there strictly by special permit, issued at the end of a long vetting procedure by the Israeli government and, for many of them, following an appeals process through the Israeli courts. You see, the full title of this commemoration is "Memorial Day for the Fallen Soldiers of the Wars of Israel and Victims of Actions of Terrorism". It's a day for Israelis, for them alone to remember whom they've lost in the struggle and to lick their wounds. As far as most of them are concerned, Palestinians are the very last people who should be here, sharing this evening with them.

That's why the protesters are here. They're enraged that Combatants United chooses to make this a joint memorial event, to remember the fallen on both sides of the struggle. On a more general level, those protesters are here to defend the status quo because they fear what will happen otherwise. But the status quo requires Israel to keep on attacking, demolishing, land-grabbing, arresting, intimidating, just to keep things in check. Seeing them up there, defending what the majority of this audience considers indefensible, Hassan decides to take his speech off-script.

"I once knew a girl who lived in Beit Sahour," he says, flicking a glance at Mohammed in the front row. "She held only love and kindness in her heart. She loved her family and friends and was always ready to help anyone. The day we met, I was a young lad on the street in need of urgent help. She was the only other person around, and she saved my life. We became good friends after that, and I got to know her well and to see her grow up. She was a happy person and never wanted anything too special – just to get married one day, raise her children, live simply and peacefully with her family around her. When the Israelis celebrated the Oslo Accords, she danced alongside them. She was thrilled with the prospect of peace at last. She had Israeli friends, people she loved very much. Can you imagine, then, what it would take to turn a sweet girl like that into a killer?"

April 2006 – The Sixth Option

This is the bus she takes to work, but work isn't her destination today. She's heading for a different part of Tel Aviv, the smart end of the business district where the city's well-heeled frequent chic restaurants, indie bookshops and smart boutiques.

Usually, she would walk to the other end of the village to catch the bus, but today she forces herself to get on at the bus stop outside her house. She makes herself look out the window as they near the school. She hasn't been down this road since the day she lost Jamila. It's morning play time, but she can't bring herself to look at the playground, to see the familiar faces, the other children, the teachers, life going on as it was. When the bus rolls over the spot where Jamila had lain lifeless, she feels the bile rising up her throat along with a scream and she clamps a hand over her mouth to keep it all down.

The bus is through the village and out on the open road before Heba lowers her hand and forces herself to takes some breaths. The day is hot, too hot, and sweat is prickling like a rash under her heavy coat. When the bus reaches the point where the roadblock had been, Heba's instinct is to turn away as she usually would, but today she forces herself to look. In her mind's eye, she sees Tariq there in the road, blood pooling around him as he pleads for help, and over there, her brother Mohammed Jr., handcuffed in the back of a jeep and powerless to come to his aid. A small wooden cross marks the spot, placed there at the side of the road by her father and brother. A rose bush has taken root next to it. Its leaves are dark green and shiny. *The water table must be high in this part of the desert*, she thinks. She wants to know who planted the bush. She wants to know whether the roses, when they bloom, will be red, yellow or pink. But it's too late. She's never going to know.

The bus draws to its final stop at the Separation Wall crossing and opens its doors to let everyone off. Heba steps down and makes her way over to the border checkpoint. Left lane for women, right lane for men. As she heads to the left, she's looking for someone in particular, the regular Tuesday guard manning the women's lane. She's friendlier than the others, she takes time to look at the faces, to say hello to the ones she recognises. And, most importantly, she waves the regulars through, saving them the indignity

of the usual frisking. *Please, please, let it be her today.* It's why
Heba's chosen a Tuesday – so much easier than a Monday,
Thursday or Friday. Even Wednesday's guard can be
unpredictable. *There she is! Tuesday's guard!* The guard sees
Heba approaching and waves her through. Heba smiles as
brightly as she can as she makes her way past, hoping the
guard doesn't spot the fear that's surely written all over her
face, or her bulky clothing on such a warm day.

Heba walks the thirty-foot length of the tunnel and
emerges into the Israeli sunshine. She scans the line of
waiting buses and makes her way over to her usual one, the
number 7 to Tel Aviv. Its route takes her past the Kings
of Israel Square, now renamed Rabin Square after the
Prime Minister who'd been assassinated there. Most days
she takes no particular interest, wrapped up in her own
thoughts, but today she looks out the window as she passes
by. Apart from an old couple sitting on a bench feeding
the pigeons, the Square is deserted. The City Hall at the
far end has an abandoned air about it. It's all in such stark
contrast to the crowds and noise that greeted her the night
she was here eleven years ago, when she'd first met Eva and
she'd sung and danced with the Israelis and believed them
when they said the violence was finished. But then one of
them that night shot their Prime Minister, the peacemaker,
and he was dead, and after that the process initiated by the
Oslo Accords eroded away to nothing, ultimately leaving
the Palestinians in a worse position than they'd ever been.

She remains seated as the bus passes her usual stop
outside the old fort on the seafront. Right next to it is the
hotel where Samuel had helped get her a job back in '94,
and where she again works. She checks her watch. Eleven
forty-five. *If they'd lived.* It's a game she plays to remind

herself of what's been taken from her, to keep the pain fresh. *If they'd lived*, Jamila would be back in her classroom after playtime, writing a story perhaps, or learning her times tables. Heba's sure that's what all her friends are busy doing, but Jamila's not with them, she's in the village cemetery. *If they'd lived*, Heba would be in the kitchen with her mother, clearing up after breakfast and making a list for her trip to the shops. Maybe she'd bump into Maha, another parent from school, and they'd stop and chat about the Roman-themed costumes they're both making for the annual school parade, and what they're planning special for the upcoming long weekend. *If they'd lived*, she'd be expecting Tariq home from the workshop for lunch, along with her father and brother, and Jamila would keep them all entertained with her lively chit-chat. That lunch table is totally diminished now, the three people still gathered around it – her mother, father and brother – unrecognisable from their former selves as they eat their meals in robotic silence.

If they'd lived, she wouldn't need to be doing any of this; her life could have carried on perfectly as it was, along its intended path. But instead, it's all been gouged out and she's been left with an empty husk. Her husband, killed; her daughter, killed; her brother, a ghost of his former self; her parents, reduced by grief; herself, thirty years old and life is over. Perhaps if it hadn't been for that army Chief of Staff and his trumped-up report, his lies and his threats, she could have found a way forward, rebuilt something from the wreckage, but he'd taken away any chance of that. When she'd said she'd handle it her own way, she'd meant it. And she'd known exactly how she'd do it. Soon after that last meeting with Samuel and Eva, she moved out of her parents' place and into a house on her own at the other end of the village. She needed the privacy to plan and prepare. She got her old job back at the hotel in Tel Aviv, and started the daily commute across the border, just like before marriage and motherhood had come along. When her parents asked why she would work for Israelis again, given what had happened, she told them she wanted to rebuild her life from a familiar place. Then they worried she was trying to go back in time, so she could forget everything that came after. But what she was doing was the opposite of forgetting – in her every waking moment, she was remembering Tariq and Jamila. What she was doing was making herself a familiar sight to the border guards, the bus driver, her fellow commuters. She'd needed to become invisible, unremarkable, preparing for the day.

She stays on the bus until it reaches the city centre where she steps down onto a crowded street. It's the lunch hour, and office workers add to the bustling scene. She stands and watches them all, looks at their faces, their clothes. They look like decent people, but they live in this bubble and they let the violence continue, a mere bus ride away, year in and year out. They need more Samuels and Evas on these streets, people who aren't afraid to challenge the status quo and call it out for what it is. It's been a comfort to know that they, at least, had troubled themselves to uncover the truth, to try to right the wrongs. It hadn't been enough, but that wasn't their fault. She certainly doesn't blame them for how it turned out. Heba knows the blame lies with people like that Chief of Staff, the scum who rise to the surface in a rotten system. He cannot go unpunished.

Eva had come looking for her a few weeks back. She'd knocked on her door and shouted for Heba to open up, she was worried about her and wanted to talk, but Heba hadn't let her in because she didn't want Eva to try to stop her. She'd received text messages from Eva after that, imploring her to respond, to meet her, to talk, to let her know if she was okay. Heba had ignored them all. What help can she be now? She's already tried and failed, hasn't she? Instead, Heba got all the help she needed from Marzen, the militant offshoot of one of the Palestinian political parties. They'd fitted her out with her explosive vest, told her where to go and when. They've been monitoring their target for weeks, and on Tuesdays at twelve-thirty she can find him entering a certain restaurant in Tel Aviv's business district, arm-in-arm with his mistress and ready to make the most of his half-day away from his desk. All she needs to do now is get on with it. They're building the Wall to stop people like her. Well, it didn't work.

She walks rapidly across the busy road, forcing cars to blast their horns and hit their brakes. One guy lowers his window and shouts at her: "Crazy bitch! Are you trying to get yourself killed?" She smiles to herself and walks on. She's aiming for the architectural water fountain on the other side of the road. It marks the entryway to a wide pedestrian boulevard that's lined with elegant two- and three-storey buildings, red-bricked and vine-laced, the homes of expensive gift shops, smart restaurants, and street cafés made cheerful with candy-stripe awnings and rambling pots of wisteria, honeysuckle and bougainvillea. Her contacts in Marzen have shown her photos – she knows exactly what it all looks like and where she's headed. She reaches the water fountain and keeps walking without breaking stride, down the middle of the boulevard, counting store fronts as she goes. There's a group of teenage schoolgirls, four or five of them, caught up in their own chatter and idly strolling in her direction. *Damn! What are they doing in this part of town?* She hadn't expected that, but there's nothing she can do about it – she's got to keep going.

Heba is fifty feet away, forty, thirty. The schoolgirls have stopped to look in a shop window. It's right next door to the restaurant. She wills them to move on, to continue up the boulevard. A sudden shout from behind makes her flinch and she resists the urge to turn around. "Hey, Izzy! Over here..." One of the girls turns, looks straight past Heba. "Hi Dad!" she shouts and raises her arm to wave. At the same moment, Heba spots the Chief of Staff walking up the boulevard arm-in-arm with his female companion. She looks like a different woman from the one in the photos, but there's no mistaking him: potbellied, bald... and in uniform. He's right on time. If only he'd been a minute or two late, the schoolgirls could have been saved. But Heba has no choice. She reaches for the cord under her coat, pulls until it is just taut, quickens her pace, twenty feet, fifteen. Her vision narrows, the sounds around her muffle. Ten, five...

As she comes alongside the Chief of Staff, she jerks the cord down, urgent. A split second passes and she thinks it's not going to work. She goes to pull the cord again. The girl Izzy glances her way. She sees her now, sees her hand on the cord, and she opens her mouth.

The explosion is violent.

The father's vision goes from twenty-twenty technicolour to blackness in an instant, like someone's turned off the television in the middle of a Walt Disney movie. But when the TV flicks back on, the channel has changed and is showing images of smoke and dust, blown-out shop fronts, and bodies strewn like rag dolls across the pavement. He staggers toward the fallen schoolgirls and drops to his knees next to the one with the guitar case strapped to her back. Izzy. He turns his daughter over, ready to gather her in his arms and rush her to the hospital. But even he can see it's no use – she's already gone.

10

Hassan

Present Day – Millennium Arena, Tel Aviv

The protestors have either heard enough and quit of their own accord or been escorted out by security; regardless, they're all gone. Hassan is winding up his speech, thanking the audience, predominantly Israeli and getting bigger each year, for choosing to remember the Palestinians too on this important day. "By being here," he tells them, "you are helping to break the silence that sustains the Occupation."

He turns to Caleb, standing beside him. His friend looks nervous so Hassan gives him a smile, squeezes his arm. "I told you earlier how we first came together, the original handful of us who set up Combatants United back in 2006," Hassan tells the audience. "This man was a stranger to me then, my supposed enemy, but he was the first Israeli I'd come across who had the guts to challenge the system and refuse to take any further part in the Occupation, choosing instead to walk a path of peace." He turns to address Caleb directly. "And by the way," he tells him, loud enough for the audience to hear, "my mother says thank you for saving her second son. If it hadn't been for you, hearing you speak your truth on TV that time, I'd have been completely lost. I'm proud to call you my brother."

April 2006 – Spilt Milk

"I'm home!" Hassan shouts, throwing his keys onto the side table in the hallway. He catches his reflection in the mirror and winces. His face is creased with dust, aging him well beyond his thirty-two years, and his hair is sweaty and flat after another day spent under a builder's helmet. He's been on the job site again, working alongside his men. The new school year starts in less than two weeks and they're racing to finish the new library at the high school over in Bethlehem. He's hot, he's tired and he badly needs a shower.

He makes his way into the kitchen where his wife Layla is scrutinising the contents of a saucepan on the hob and looking less than pleased. This is why his mother takes care of breakfast and lunch, and he takes over the cooking at the weekends: Layla is good at many things, but cooking is not one of them.

"Smells great," he says, giving her a kiss on the cheek. "Mother's quiet. Is she here?" He's used to hearing her from the living room when he gets home, providing a running commentary of the evening's news to Layla, who's generally shouting back exactly what she thinks about it all. As he often tells them, their neighbours don't need TVs with those two keeping them up-to-date with what's going on in the world. But today his mother is unusually quiet. Hassan sticks his head around the door to check on her and sees a harrowing sight. His mother is sat frozen to the television, her fists scrunched against her face in anguish.

"Mother, what's wrong?" he says. "What's upset you?"

"There's been another one," she replies, nodding toward the television.

Hassan looks at the screen and sees a reporter standing next to a water fountain at the top end of a street. It looks like one of those smart pedestrian ones you find in Israeli cities, Haifa perhaps or, more likely, Tel Aviv. On any other day, this would be an elegant spot, but today the scene behind the reporter is one of utter devastation. Tables and chairs are strewn across the sidewalk, upturned, smashed, destroyed; blown-in shop fronts gape open-mouthed; awnings hang in shreds from mangled frames; a bronze statue has toppled over, its face crushed against a bench; and there's glass and debris everywhere. People wearing the uniforms of first responders are buzzing all over the place, putting up a cordon to keep back onlookers, scouring the ground, taking photos and writing notes. This is the aftermath of a horrific explosion. The ambulances must have already been and gone, because Hassan can't see any signs of casualties. He notices a shoe in a tree, dangling by a lace – a white trainer with a green stripe. He wills someone to look up, to retrieve it.

"Suicide bombing in Tel Aviv," his mother says. "A woman this time."

"Is that why you're crying, Mother? Because it's a woman?" Hassan knows she's seen reports of suicide bombers on the news recently. Who hasn't? Palestinians pushed to their absolute limit who blow themselves up along with as many Israelis as possible. It's horrible, but it's never brought her to tears before.

"I'm crying because of the children," she says.

He turns to the television and reads the headlines scrolling across the bottom of the screen: *Army Chief of*

Staff targeted and killed in suicide bombing attack. At least eight civilians among the fatalities, including five girls from Tel Aviv High School. Bomber confirmed to be female. Further details expected shortly.

"Mother, the dead are all Israeli!" Hassan is surprised by his mother's reaction. It's not that she doesn't have a heart, but after all the suffering she's endured, she's surely more sparing these days about whom she chooses to grieve? "You've already cried a lifetime of tears over our own kids. Come on, stop now."

"Palestinian, Israeli, they're all children," she replies. "Do you think those poor girls' parents are feeling the pain any less than I did when Karim was killed? No, they're not!"

Hassan crosses the room and sits next to his mother. He takes her hand, but doesn't speak. He's not sure, yet, what to say.

"They interviewed the girls' teacher just now," his mother continues. "The five of them had their own rock band and wanted to be famous one day. Karim was the same, wasn't he? It was just him and his guitar, of course, but he always said he would be a pop star."

Karim, Hassan's kid brother. He'd be thirty now if he were still alive, but he didn't make it past thirteen.

Hassan looks back at the TV and catches the tail-end of a news flash as it scrolls along the bottom of the screen: *...named as Heba El-Issa, widowed Beit Sahour woman.*

Heba? What's she doing in the news? Not for one moment does it occur to Hassan that there might be a connection between the coverage of the suicide bombing they're watching and the text beneath it. *It must be something to do with her daughter's death,* he thinks.

It's his mother who's the first to realise. "*She* did it!" she gasps, slapping a hand over her mouth in shock. "That lovely girl who used to give you milk! I don't believe it!"

"No, it can't be!" Hassan says, but his mother's right. The news flash is playing on a loop and Hassan sees the full dreadful bulletin as it comes back around: *Suicide bomber in today's attack named as Heba El-Issa, widowed Beit Sahour woman.*

"But she wouldn't do that," is all Hassan can manage as he stares at the screen. This is the girl who'd hid him in the hay and ran to fetch the doctor when he'd dislocated his shoulder escaping that sadistic bastard, Ice, back in '89. The Beit Sahour dairy had become a regular night-time spot for Hassan and his gang after that. Soft hay to sleep on and hide in, cows to keep the place warm, and as a special bonus, if he was still there when Heba and her father arrived in the mornings, he'd be given milk and eggs to drop home to his family in the refugee camp.

Then came the terrible morning his family's life had been torn apart. Hassan had just arrived home from a night spent at the dairy. He planned to quickly drop off the eggs and milk Heba had given him and then leave again for another day with the gang, but as he walked in through the front door the sirens sounded around the Camp, signalling an unexpected curfew.

His mother rushed into the hallway, relieved to see him home before the soldiers were out patrolling the streets. She took the milk and eggs from him and headed back to the kitchen, calling to his brother as she went, "Karim, come quickly. Take some of this to your uncle. Goodness knows how long we're going to be locked down and we can't have him starving to death."

Karim dashed out the front door with a cup of milk and half-dozen eggs, along with his mother's behest: "Come straight back!"

"Okay," he replied. And that was it. A few moments later, the sound of gunfire pierced the air and Hassan had somehow known. He rushed to the front door and looked down the alley toward his uncle's house. There was Karim, just feet away, sprawled facedown in the dirt with two bullet wounds in the centre of his back. Bizarrely, Hassan's brain spent a moment lamenting the smashed eggs and spilt milk before acknowledging the fact his brother was dead. When he turned to look for the source of the gunfire, it was Ice he saw standing at the top of the alley. He sneered at Hassan before turning around and casually walking away.

Despite his urgent need for revenge, Hassan had had to give up his rabble-rousing way of life after that. With his father away on business trips so often, someone was needed at home to take care of his mother. She'd always been the strong one in the family, the one to hold them all together when things went wrong, pushing them all forward. But after Karim's death, she suffered what the doctor called a "nervous breakdown". She needed looking after, and part of that was making sure he kept himself safe. His mother couldn't stand the worry of him being out on the streets twenty-four hours a day, at risk of becoming another Ice victim. He gave up the gang, handed the mantle over to Amir, and moved back home. With curfews keeping school closed much of the time, he went to work on a construction site and, except for one run-in with Ice that led to a six-month stint in juvenile prison, he managed to keep himself out of trouble. When his father died of a heart attack a couple years later, Hassan had become solely responsible for taking care of his mother. The two have lived together in the family home ever since, and when he married Layla, she moved in with them. Somehow, by living their lives simply and quietly over the years, they've managed to find some peace.

Now, sitting there on the sofa and holding his mother's hand as her tears continue to fall, Hassan feels everything inside him shift and slide. His mother's grief, still unspent after all these years. His own guilt – for bringing Ice to their door; for causing his brother's death – still unspoken. The old anger. The need for action. It's roiling up inside. All this death and suffering. When will it end? He's got to do something. But what?

Two days later, these thoughts are still troubling Hassan when a different news story out of Israel grabs his attention. This time, it's about five young conscripts in the Israeli army, eighteen- and nineteen-year olds, who have just written to their Prime Minister to say they are no longer willing to serve in the Occupied Palestinian Territories. According to the newscaster, they had been ordered to attend a cave community located ten kilometres south of Hebron where the Palestinian inhabitants "were becoming violent toward their Israeli neighbours" living in the nearby settlement. "The five soldiers, who have now been discharged from the army, refused to attend, despite being aware the Palestinians posed a significant risk to the safety of the settlers," she continues. "They're known as "refuseniks", soldiers who derogate from their duty to defend our country, and I have one of them here with me in the studio to explain what they were hoping to achieve through their actions."

The newscaster proceeds to give the poor boy such a roasting, Hassan begins to feel sorry for him. The public are given the opportunity to call in with their comments whilst the interview's on air. It's brutal. The young man gets called a traitor by one angry caller, told he's disgraceful and no longer a true Israeli by another. The least threatening call is from an elderly lady who offers prayers for his poor suffering family. But the insubordinate soldier manages to stay calm as he tries to explain his point of view. He says something about being proud to be Israeli, blah, blah, blah, but then he goes on to say something that really catches Hassan's attention: "I am sorry if my actions offend you," he says, looking directly into the camera, "but during my short time in the army, I saw enough to know I could no longer be a part of it: this system of oppression and brutality we use to keep ourselves *secure* and our Palestinian neighbours *in check*. The continued occupation of Palestine is a moral stain on our nation and needs to end. The *disgraceful* ones here are those among us who close their eyes and refuse to see what's going on."

Wow! Hassan has never heard an Israeli speak like this before. *He really sees what's happening, and he detests it,* he thinks.

"What about the recent spate of suicide bombers coming across the border?" the newscaster asks. "Like the one just two days ago – the Palestinian woman who murdered a top army officer and several civilians, including five schoolgirls."

"I agree, it's horrific," he tells her, "but if you want to understand why that happens, you need to go to the Occupied Territories in person and see for yourself what we are doing to these people."

When the interview is over, Hassan knows he's got his new direction. He will find this young man and talk to him, and together they will find everyone else who sees things as they do, and then they will become a force for change.

11

Caleb

A few seconds from now, there's going to be total silence and Caleb's going to have to start talking. He hasn't spoken in public since that nightmare of a television interview sixteen years ago. Hassan is looking at him expectantly. The audience is growing quiet and all eyes are on him. He fears that when he opens his mouth, no words are going to come out. He goes to pull his speech out of his pocket, but it's not there – all his trouser pockets are empty. He scans the floor around him, thinking maybe it's fallen out, but it's not there either. Then realisation hits and his heart begins to hammer in his chest. The speech is in his jacket pocket – the jacket that he left backstage because he was too hot.

Silence falls and Caleb stands rooted to the spot. Can he quickly dash off the stage to retrieve his speech? No. He's going to have to talk from memory. How does his speech start, again? What was the first sentence? He'd recited it in his head just a few minutes ago.

Oh god, I've forgotten the whole thing!

Noticing Caleb's hesitancy, Hassan steps back up to the mic. "The last time this guy spoke out, he was treated like the enemy. Let's show him he's among friends this time."

Given the very different lives the two of them have led up to this point – his one of ease and privilege, Hassan's one of adversity and loss – Caleb is doubly grateful for Hassan's support in this moment. Yes, they're both founding members of Combatants United, and they're both here tonight doing their part for the greater cause, but their reasons couldn't be more different. For Caleb, it's been a route to personal absolution, a form of therapy for his moral injury, a matter of ethical choice. But Hassan is still going through his troubles every single day. The harassment, the indignity, the absence of freedom, the violence, the reality of living under the Occupation. *Fuck, get over yourself, Caleb!* He takes a breath, steps up to the mic and begins.

"One day long ago, I got a call from my friend Hassan here. I thought it was someone else calling, someone I'd been waiting to hear from." Caleb pauses, looks around the arena. "Come to think of it, I'm still waiting for that person to contact me." This earns a few chuckles from the audience, as Caleb casts his eyes everywhere except on the front row. "But I digress," he continues. "The day Hassan called, I was probably the most despised person in Israel. I'd followed a course of action I believed to be correct, but almost everyone else disagreed. I was at the lowest point of my life. This evening, I want to tell you about that."

April 2006 – Hero to Traitor in under a Year

When Caleb receives that call, he's back at his family's home on the kibbutz, licking his wounds and trying to figure out what's next for him. It's hard to believe it was less than a year ago he'd packed his kit bag and gone off to join the most elite army unit in Israel, feeling so sure of himself, so proud. When he'd been selected at sixteen, the first from his kibbutz to make the grade, he'd felt special. Not once did he or anyone else doubt he was bound for heroic greatness, and when the day had come, his first posting – straight to the Occupied Territories, no less – the kibbutz had thrown a party to see him off. He'd be serving for all of them: his country, his community and his family.

Caleb's grandfather had arrived on the shores of Palestine back in 1946, just after the end of the Second World War, age thirteen and on his own. He'd been liberated from a concentration camp in Poland by the Brits and put on a boat headed for his people's "homeland". His parents and two siblings had perished during the previous winter, succumbing to starvation and illness. Soon after his arrival, he was fostered by a family who themselves had come by boat from Europe back in 1918.

When the State of Israel was declared in 1948, Caleb's grandfather was told it was "a land without a people for a people without a land". Indeed, for him, it was sanctuary. He grew up in Tel Aviv well cared for, educated and healthy, met his future wife at the garment factory where they both worked, married, and had a son, Caleb's father.

And then in 1967, the Six Day War resulted in Israel seizing control of the West Bank, along with other nearby Arab territories, and holding them under military occupation. Five years later, when there was no sign of the Occupation ending any time soon, Caleb's grandparents took their son and joined several other young Israeli families pioneering a new form of living off the land in the

West Bank, to settle it and lay permanent claim to it. They established a moshav, a form of cooperative farming where families were allotted their own land to farm, but pooled their produce to sell at market. They brought modern farming methods to the West Bank – machinery, plastic greenhouse tenting, chemicals. They grew vegetables, grapes and other fruits. They kept cows, sheep, goats and chickens. They brought young volunteers from the United States and Europe to help work the land and feel part of their worthy cause. Most significantly, they believed in a "beneficial occupation": that the Palestinians could benefit from having Israeli settlements like theirs inhabit their land. They provided employment opportunities to the Palestinians living in surrounding villages – initially, in helping to build these new settlements, and then later through labouring in their fields. They believed the two peoples, the settlers and the Palestinians, could live side-by-side to their mutual benefit. Caleb's grandparents believed, in fact, in helping their Palestinian hosts to prosper, and to see them develop their own industries. In 1989 they bartered eighteen cows for twelve goats and three dozen chickens with the nearby Palestinian village of Beit Sahour, which was eager to establish its own dairy farm. They'd been pleased to cooperate, but all that goodwill toward their neighbours began to evaporate as the First Intifada wore on. As they saw it, the Palestinians were throwing all the help back in the Israelis' faces and becoming rebellious, refusing to pay their taxes, and resisting what they saw as harsh treatment by the Israeli army.

Caleb's father was twenty-seven years old and married by now with a two-year-old Caleb, living with his wife and her family on a kibbutz deep in the Israeli countryside. The paternal grandparents gave up their life on the West Bank moshav and moved to the kibbutz, for the security that came with living within the borders of Israel.

Caleb remembers his idyllic upbringing on the kibbutz, surrounded by a full complement of parents and grandparents, and beyond that, the community around them, all looking out for each other, pulling together, farming the land, sharing the yield, eating together in the vast communal dining hall. Caleb had grown up in innocence, with his nose stuck in a book when he wasn't feeding the chickens or helping pick crops. It was a way of life worth defending.

Everyone who came before him, and everyone around him then, had done their duty for their country. Now it was his turn. When the kibbutz came out in force to send him off to the army as their home-grown hero, his mother and father couldn't have looked more proud. And he was ready. He was straining at the leash. Of course he was! He'd gone through two years of special training to ensure that. Plus he'd made the school trip to the concentration camps of Poland and seen first-hand what had happened there. So he'd understood that his people are "the Persecuted", under continual threat of annihilation, that they are "the Chosen Ones", to whom this whole land rightfully belongs, that it was his job to defend his precious Israel from existential threat, from the Palestinians who want to throw them all into the sea and take the land for themselves.

He was pumped with a lethal cocktail of hatred, fear, inexperience, naivety and teenage hormones, and he was ready for action.

The unravelling of his heroic mission, what he'll eventually come to see as the start of his enlightenment, had begun last October, the day at Khaybar Caves when he'd shot his rifle and the bullet had ended up in that Palestinian man's head. He still can't understand how it happened, how despite aiming for the ground, the man had ended up laying lifeless in the dirt, his face a bloodied mess. Was he dead? Caleb didn't know – they hadn't stayed to find out. The commander had ordered them all back into the jeep as soon as it had happened and they'd left, returning along the rutted track after a job "well done".

Back at base that evening, Caleb's shock had turned to anger and he'd lashed out at Ethan, his assigned partner that day. "Why didn't you shoot when the commander ordered you to?" Caleb snarled at him.

"Why did *you*?" Ethan snapped back angrily. "They were only trying to save their belongings from being torched by the settlers. We should have been helping them, keeping the settlers away, not attacking them ourselves. I told you, this army isn't about defending Israel, it's about erasing Palestine and all its people. Ethnic cleansing, that's our job here."

Caleb stared at Ethan, trying to remain angry with him, but instead he was shocked to realise he agreed with him. "I know," he said eventually. "I can't believe I'm saying this, but what we were ordered to do today was wrong. I thought we were supposed to be fighting terrorists, but they were just ordinary people..."

Ethan nodded.

"What do you think happened to that guy?" Caleb continued, frowning with concern. "Do you think he survived? Got to a hospital?"

"How would we know? We just left him there!"

"And we're supposed to be the *World's Most Moral Army*?" Caleb said. "What a sick joke."

Over the next few weeks, Caleb and Ethan constantly revisited the events of that day, questioning the rights and wrongs of what happened, what they would do if ordered to do it again, if there was a next time. Then one night in the canteen after dinner, the topic got picked up for general debate by the soldiers around the table. This was not an easy thing for them to be discussing. Every one of them there, when entering the army, had sworn an oath of loyalty to their country and to their commanders. Just talking about the possibility of having doubts felt seditious. But everyone had had a couple of beers by this point, and tongues were loosened as a result. Most of the guys ribbed Caleb and Ethan for their consciences, accused them of being yellow-bellies, but at least five or six of them seemed to agree that what they'd been ordered to do at the Caves was wrong.

That's when Caleb and Ethan drafted their letter, to have it ready in case there was a next time. Soon enough, their commander came into the canteen one morning as they were finishing breakfast and told them they were going back to Khaybar. The cave dwellers were playing up again, this time because the Ministry of Defence had declared some of their fields a *Special Military Zone* and were denying them access to their crops. They needed to go over there and take care of the situation.

"No!" Caleb said, rising from his chair. "I won't do it! Not again."

Ethan rose from his chair, too. "I won't either."

"You think you get to cherry pick the missions you go out on?" the commander roared.

"We won't help with denying Palestinians access to their land," Caleb told him. "That's all they have to live on."

A third soldier rose from his chair, then a fourth and a fifth. The five of them stood facing the commander in stony defiance, while the others remained firmly seated.

"Every one of you, be at the vehicles and ready to depart at zero eight hundred hours and I'll forget this ever happened," the commander snarled before storming out.

The five dissenters remained glued to their spots while all the other soldiers filed briskly out of the canteen, eager to obey their commander's orders.

"Now what?" said one of the five when they were alone.

"It's time to make our stand," Caleb replied. "Ethan and I have prepared a letter..."

"I'll go and get it," said Ethan, dashing out. When he came back into the canteen he was carrying an envelope, from which he pulled out a handwritten letter addressed to *The Prime Minister of Israel*. No point doing things by halves, they'd decided.

"Read it," encouraged Caleb.

"*Sir*," Ethan started, clearing his throat. "*On entering the army, we believed its purpose was to defend Israel. We now believe that Israel needs to be defended because of its army. We shall no longer assist in the occupation of Palestine. We shall no longer take part in depriving millions of Palestinians their basic human rights. We shall no longer corrupt our moral character in missions of oppression. We shall no longer deny our responsibility as soldiers of the Israeli Defence Force.*"

"It's good," said Caleb, grabbing a pen and being the first to scrawl his signature along the bottom of the letter. Ethan was quick to sign next, before offering the pen to the others. "Who else?" he asked.

Zero eight hundred hours that morning found the five of them in the canteen drinking coffee, their letter handed off to the cook along with a one hundred shekel note. The letter was to be hand-delivered to the Prime Minister's office in Jerusalem that morning; the cash was for a photocopy to be made of it first, for dropping off at the TV news studios on the way. For his efforts, the cook was happy to "keep the change".

And that's how Caleb along with four others in his unit became refuseniks. They weren't the first, and they wouldn't be the last. There had been refuseniks during the First Intifada in the '80s and early '90s, outspoken in their refusal to trade bullets for rocks on Palestinian streets, pilloried as radicals and traitors and given long stints in military prisons to reflect on their ideals. Other refuseniks have found more discreet ways to avoid active service – turning up at the draft centre with a note from a psychiatrist diagnosing them as psychologically unfit for combat duty, or simply telling their commander they don't want to serve in the Occupied Palestinian Territories – getting themselves quietly assigned to desk jobs instead. But Caleb and his peers wanted their refusal to be a catalyst for change, and for that it had to be as loud and as public as possible.

The midday news opened with live scenes from Khaybar Caves in the hills south of Hebron, the reporter on scene explaining the events of the morning that had led up to the olive trees behind her, blackened and still smouldering, being set on fire. Earlier that day, she explained, a number of soldiers from the nearby army barracks had refused to attend when called out to protect a military zone from Palestinian aggressors who were trying to break down the security barriers and trespass on the land. Because of the refuseniks' dereliction of duty, the attending army unit was left severely undermanned and it had taken the assistance of nearby settlers to clear the Palestinians away, setting fire to the olive trees to root them out.

Caleb and the others watched on in open-mouthed horror as the reporter handed back to the studio and the newscaster, sitting calmly at her desk with their letter to the Prime Minister on full and magnified display on the screen behind her, proceeded to read its contents, followed by the names of the five signatories before reporting that the soldiers in question were currently in lockdown at their base pending yet-to-be-determined disciplinary action.

As soon as the news segment finished, their phones sprang to life – the ringing, dinging and pinging of girlfriends, mothers and fathers, pals from the gym, neighbours, everyone it seemed, wanting to know if it was really them, was it true, what on earth did they think they were doing? Caleb's most supportive call was from his grandfather, who told him, "I can't agree with what you're doing, but if it truly comes from the heart, I will respect it."

The media loves a good story, especially one that whips up the emotional pulse of the nation into a high state of outrage, and this one was perfect. For three days straight, television stations and newspapers all across Israel hounded after the flesh and blood of the Hebron Refuseniks, harassing their families for exclusive interviews, tracking down old school teachers for stories of early insurrection, offering money to their friends in exchange for photos and comments. The fact they were serving soldiers and had gone straight to the top in such a public way had provoked a real backlash. They were being talked about all over Israel – in its coffee shops, on the buses, in offices and on factory floors. They were being called traitors and cowards. They'd become notorious. This was frustrating in the extreme for Caleb and his fellow refuseniks, because throughout all of this they had no means of giving their side of the story, of explaining their actions. They were still holed up in barracks and could only sit by and watch, their sense of injustice mounting by the day. Surely, if they got to speak, nobody could disagree with them? What they'd been ordered to do to those people was inhumane.

Eventually, the judgment came down: they must remove their names from the letter within a week or they would be dishonourably discharged from the army. None of them did. They were all dishonourably discharged. At least now they were free to tell their side of the story, and this was when Caleb had agreed to do that live television interview, the one that had caught Hassan's attention. To have the wrath of ordinary people directed at you like that had been a bizarre experience. It felt like it was happening to a different Caleb – he still loved his country and his family, his friends, his life on the kibbutz, but how, then, could nobody else who is part of that life see things in the same way as him? He told the interviewer, "I am still the proud Israeli I always was, the difference is that I now see we can be better than this. If you are not against the Occupation, you are for it, because you let it go on. Personally, I don't want to wonder twenty years from now why I didn't do anything."

The problem was, he had no idea where to go next with his new-found beliefs. He was out of the army and out of favour. He tried discussing things with his parents and friends back on the kibbutz, but they didn't get it. It was his duty to serve, they said. He was following orders when he shot his rifle, they said. The bigger cause was worth the casualties, they said. And, they said, things are complex – that easy excuse, so often trotted out to blur the picture – but in Caleb's mind, it was simple: his country's occupation of Palestine had to end.

A week after the television interview, once the media had moved on from the Hebron Refuseniks scandal and had dropped the five of them back down to earth, Caleb decided to return to Khaybar to look for the man he'd left for dead. It felt like the obvious place to start on this path to redemption, or enlightenment, or whatever it was. Ethan and the other refuseniks joined him. They took clothing and bedding, cans of food, toys for the kids, even some egg-laying chickens. They found the guy's parents easily enough, but they were scared to have Israelis turn up like this, even ones wearing jeans and T-shirts. While the others unloaded their gifts from the back of the car, Caleb showed the parents the front page of a newspaper carrying a photo of him beneath the word "Traitor". Wary still, their hosts nonetheless beckoned the five of them into their cave and served them hot tea. Sitting there on the floor, Caleb explained how upset they'd been about the incident with their son, and how it had led them to becoming refuseniks. He said he was very concerned to know how their son was, to offer an apology. In reply, the parents told Caleb he'd gone away, they didn't know where, exactly; his visits home nowadays were brief, sporadic; he was angry about what was happening to his community; he couldn't live there any longer, doing nothing but sit and wait for the next attack. At least Caleb now knew the guy had survived the shooting – he'd dreaded being told he had died from his wounds, or finding him at the Caves but permanently maimed. His name was Omar. Caleb left a note for him, together with his phone number and a request that he call.

That was two weeks ago, and he really shouldn't be disheartened that Omar hasn't contacted him yet. But still, Caleb's need to speak with him, to say sorry, to be given permission to lay his guilt to rest, is a constant torment. He went to a psychiatrist last week and got himself a label for what he's feeling: *moral injury,* that is to say, according to his encyclopaedia, "an injury to an individual's moral conscience and values resulting from an act of perceived moral transgression, which produces profound emotional guilt and shame, and in some cases also a sense of betrayal, anger and profound moral disorientation". What it boils down to, is Caleb needs to speak to Omar, and as soon as possible.

This is why, when his phone rings now and he sees it's a West Bank number, Caleb grabs it up and urgently jabs at the flashing green square. But the caller is an older man, introducing himself as Hassan. He says he was active in the First Intifada, a rebel out on the streets, doing his best to fight the Israeli army, but nowadays he's committed to a peaceful life. He tells Caleb that he saw him on the news recently, talking about becoming a refusenik, and decided to track him down. He and a couple of his friends are interested in meeting Caleb and two other Israelis they've heard about, to see if they can join forces in some way. Caleb is sceptical, suspicious, but agrees it's worth a try. They arrange to meet the following Sunday at the El Capitan Hotel.

12

Eva

Present Day – Millennium Arena, Tel Aviv

Eva knows who Caleb means when he says he's waiting to hear from someone: he means Omar. She glances across at Omar as Caleb says it, interested in his reaction, but he doesn't flinch. She's got to agree it's weird, the guy's been a member of Combatants United for three years now and he still hasn't spoken to Caleb, the man who with a single wayward bullet, sent his life spiralling off track. Not only has Omar not spoken to Caleb, he seems to actively avoid him, sticking to the other end of the room, or field, or wherever they happen to be, always making sure he's keeping some distance between them. Everyone's wondering what's going on there. For better or worse, Caleb's had such a massive impact on Omar's life, surely he's got something to say to him?

She feels bad for Caleb – after seventeen years of waiting, he deserves to get closure from Omar. She's been rooting for Caleb since the day they first met and he told her he was looking for a Palestinian from Khaybar named Omar and asked if she might know of him. She replied unfortunately no, and went on to say how pleased she was to meet him, she was so impressed with what he'd done, a new recruit in the army and he'd had the balls to make a stand like that; she wished more conscripts would do the same; hell, she wished she'd done it when she'd had the chance. And she'd given Caleb a hug then, because from the look on his face he didn't hear this sort of thing often enough.

Eva remembers that day especially well because it was also the day that she, Caleb and Samuel went off to meet with three Palestinians over in Bethlehem, apparently to talk about them "not being combatants anymore". At that point, she still hadn't made up her mind whether it was an act of brilliance or lunacy on her part, whether the three of them could trust the word of their Palestinian hosts or if they were walking into a trap.

May 2006 – Six Combatants Come Face-to-Face

Eva has been to the El Capitan Hotel before, several times in fact, in the line of her work. Since she knows the way, she's been given the job of navigating. Samuel's behind the wheel and Caleb's in the back. They're all feeling on edge. None of them are strangers to the West Bank, but this time they've arranged to meet three Palestinians in private. Eva's mind is all over the place, aflutter with white doves one moment and flooded with fear the next. She's done her research on the main guy, Hassan, digging up everything she can about him. She found a news story dating back to the First Intifada. He was living in Aida Camp then, and Eva assumes he's still there now since it's a place very few people leave. It's just a kilometre or two up the road from the hotel, so if he has moved, it can't have been far. The story she'd read about him was not an unfamiliar one. Hassan's younger brother had died when an Israeli soldier shot him in "self-defence" one night during a curfew in the Camp. The family said afterward the boy had been on his way to his uncle's house, that he had nothing to do with making trouble for the soldiers. The army's word against the word of the bereaved family? Eva knows whose version her money's on – look what happened when Jamila was killed. Knowing about Hassan's brother makes her feel she has a point of connection with him. She wants to trust him, to believe this meeting is about rapprochement and not revenge.

They cross the border without a hitch, their Israeli plates and identity papers getting them waved through the checkpoint with hardly a second glance. They're now on the outskirts of Bethlehem, on the road that will take them to the hotel. Everything looks very peaceful, just as it should on a Sunday morning here. There are more pigeons than people on the sidewalks and the traffic is light. When Eva hears a motorbike coming up fast behind them and glances around to look, the faces of the two lads staring back reveal only curiosity.

Suddenly, a young boy steps into the road in front of them and puts up a hand for them to stop. "What the heck?" Samuel slams on the brakes and they skid to a halt. The boy, who's maybe ten or eleven years old, walks toward the driver's side of the vehicle and Samuel lowers his window an inch, just enough to hear what he has to say.

"This road is closed," the boy tells Samuel. Three smaller kids walk up and stand behind him. Eva's notices they're all very nicely dressed in long trousers and collared shirts, and their faces are clean, their hair neatly combed. One of them is carrying a homemade *stop* sign, a thick red line painted across a sheet of card, which he now hoists above his head.

"See?" he says, giving them a cheeky grin. Eva looks around but can't see any traffic police or anyone else official-looking. "Our brother's getting married and the reception's going to be up there," the bigger boy says, pointing up the road. "You need to go around the back way. You go down there," he says, pointing now to a narrow side road, "then go right, then right again where the bakery is, and you get back on this road further up."

"Thanks, that's very helpful of you," Samuel says, closing his window. He turns to look at Eva and Caleb. "Well? What do you think?"

"Let me call Hassan," Caleb says, pulling his phone from his pocket. "If this is a setup, I'll hear it in his voice." Caleb gets through to Hassan and asks him about a wedding, whether they need to take a detour. "Okay," he says, after a few moments, "then we'll see you soon." He disconnects and slides the phone back into his pocket. "He says he knows about the wedding. If we want to avoid going around the backstreets, he suggests we turn around and come in from the other direction, but that will add about thirty minutes to the trip." Caleb pauses. "For what it's worth, he sounded genuine."

"I guess if he *was* planning some sort of ambush, he'd have pushed us to take the backstreets," Eva says.

"Yes, and they're already at the hotel waiting for us. I say we take the detour."

Just at that moment, they hear music – pulsating drums, a lively flute, clanging cymbals – mixed with the sound of cheering and shouting. There's a throng of people filling up the road behind them, coming their way, and effectively forcing their decision. "Looks like a wedding party to me," Caleb says, turning to face the front. "There's no way we can turn around and go back that way now. The road is totally blocked."

"Okay," Samuel says, putting the car into gear. "Let's get this over with."

He's just pulling away when there's a series of loud bangs from behind them, making them all jump. Samuel chuckles. "Firecrackers!" he says. "You'd think they'd prefer something that didn't sound like gunfire, wouldn't you!"

Ten minutes later, they're driving into the hotel car park. They make their way to the reception desk and ask for Hassan. Eva recognises the receptionist from previous visits to the hotel and is again struck by her resemblance to Heba in the early days. It's the long dark hair, the fringe framing her face like a child's, her bubbly nature, like nothing's going to spoil her day. "Of course, they're just through there," the receptionist says cheerfully, pointing to a doorway behind them. "Go on through."

Caleb knocks tentatively and pokes his head around the door. Voices, friendly sounding, respond with "Hi!" and "Please, come on in". They're greeted by three men, who get up from the table as they enter. One of them steps forward and offers his hand to Caleb. He's heavily built, and an intimidating presence until he smiles. "Hassan," he says. "It's good to meet you. Thank you for coming." The other two men step forward and introduce themselves as Amir and Fayez. They're more guarded than Hassan, their welcome for the Israelis a little cooler. Hassan is quick to explain they're all neighbours from Aida Camp, in fact they've known each other all their lives. Amir and Fayez nod along, smiling at their friend. *They're just shy*, Eva tells herself.

With the introductions done, Hassan invites everyone to take a seat, suggesting they arrange themselves Israeli-Palestinian-Israeli. "We're not adversaries here, setting up for a negotiation," he says. "We should all sit together as friends."

Once everyone's seated, Eva takes a moment to look around the room. It's much like the rest of the hotel: clean but basic. Nothing adorns the off-white walls; the single window, bare of curtains or blinds, looks on to an empty courtyard. A vase of plastic flowers – pink peonies – sits in the middle of the table in a forlorn attempt at cheerfulness. Hassan pours them water and coffee, and asks if they're hungry, would they like anything to eat? They assure him they're fine with the coffee and water, thanks, and then there's nothing left but to make a start. Hassan places his hands flat on the table and looks around at them all. "We have all been combatants, fighting on opposite sides of the struggle," he begins, "and now we each understand that fighting solves nothing, it leads only to more fighting. We all deserve to live in peace, but we have to find a different way to get there."

Eva feels reassured by his words, intrigued to know what he's got in mind.

"It has to start with dialogue," Hassan continues, "on a big scale I mean, involving many thousands of people on each side. But it can begin with the six of us here, in this room today. Let's try to understand each other, what we each want, hear each other's stories. I think we'll see we're not so very different. We're former adversaries, we're strangers, but I believe – I hope – we'll soon be partners. Think of the power of that message, what we can achieve if we work together."

Hassan pauses, takes a sip of water. "Caleb, we're all here because I saw you on television talking about why you became a refusenik. If you don't mind, why don't you tell us more about that?"

So, Caleb tells his story, from his idyllic childhood growing up on the kibbutz, to his pride in being selected to join an elite army unit, to then being ordered to set upon an innocent community when he'd injured a man, to finally making the decision to refuse when he was ordered to do it again. He concludes by telling everyone how surprising it's been, to think of himself as an average Israeli, only to discover how differently he sees the world from everyone around him: his family, friends, community. He's finding company among strangers lately, he says – first his fellow refuseniks, and now the five other people sitting with him around this table.

There's silence when he's finished. Everyone's thoughtful, and Caleb's looking serious too, until he suddenly lets out a yelp. "I just remembered!" he says with a grimace. "I have to make a call."

While he's on the phone, Eva explains to their hosts how nervous they'd been about meeting them today, so nervous, in fact, they'd arranged with one of Caleb's friends to raise the alarm if they didn't report in by noon. Hassan looks at his watch. "It's okay, no need for us terrorists to run for the hills," he says, breaking into a grin. "It's only eleven-fifty."

Eva likes this guy, he's a thinker, he seems sensible and has a friendly manner. She can see that Samuel and Caleb feel comfortable with him, too. "Why don't you tell us your story next, Hassan?" she says. She wants to hear what he has to say about his brother's shooting, to see, in his telling of it, what he reveals about blame. That will help her decide whether he's being straight with them when he talks about peace.

Hassan proceeds to tell the group that his brother was shot and killed by an Israeli soldier in 1989. "But that's not really what brought me here today," he says, going on to explain how he'd come home from work a few weeks ago to find his mother crying over the news about a group of schoolgirls in Tel Aviv who'd been killed by a suicide bomber. "Someone high up in the army had been the main target – the kids were just in the wrong place at the wrong time. She said she was crying for the kids' parents, that it was like when we lost Karim, and I saw she was right. Israeli children, Palestinian children. Israeli parents, Palestinian parents. It makes no difference, it's the same thing. This isn't a war we're in, with our two armies fighting the battle for us – this is normal people, our two communities pitted against each other, killing each other. Generations after generations of us, fearing and hating the "enemy". And I realised we shouldn't be fighting each other, we should be coming together to fight the system that's put us here. Then I saw Caleb on the news, saying the same things I was thinking." Hassan pauses here, looks at the faces around the table, before proceeding. "I knew the bomber, by the way," he says. "Her family ran the dairy in Beit Sahour during the First Intifada; she used to give me milk and eggs to take back to the Camp. She was always so happy, full of life. Finding out that it was her, someone I knew and admired – well, it was a real shock."

"You knew Heba? Me too!" Eva says, surprising even herself. The faces looking back at her are wide-eyed. Only Samuel knows about her connection with Heba and she looks at him questioningly. He nods, encouraging her to go on. "The suicide bomber that Hassan just told us about, she was my friend," she says. "I didn't expect to be talking about her today – I thought I'd be telling you about my work as a journalist, my anti-Occupation reporting, but after listening to Hassan, I feel I should give you my angle on the story."

"Wow, how amazing is that?" Hassan says, looking pleased. "Heba was your friend too! Go on, tell us more. How did you know her?"

Eva starts at the end, the moment she learned what Heba had done in Tel Aviv. "I was probably watching the same channel as you and your mother, Hassan. I was appalled, seeing the devastation and carnage, listening to the details of fatalities and injuries. And then I saw it scrolling along the bottom of the screen: *Suicide bomber in today's attack named as Heba El-Issa, widowed Beit Sahour woman.*" These last words come out as a sob and Samuel takes her hand, gives it a squeeze. "I met her the night of Rabin's assassination – we were in the Square together when he was shot," Eva continues. "She was so happy to be there, celebrating the Oslo Accords shoulder-to-shoulder with Israelis. I believe we met on one of the happiest nights of her life, because it all went terribly wrong after that."

Eva goes on to explain how Heba's husband had died after being shot by an Israeli soldier at a checkpoint, and then how her young daughter, Jamila, had been shot outside her school and the army investigation into her death had been a series of lies to protect the soldier responsible, and how she and Samuel had tried to help, to expose the truth, but they saw they were only going to make things worse.

"I struggle to say Heba was right... how can killing people ever be right?" Eva says. "But I understand how she got to that point. She'd lost the two people she lived for, both of them murdered, and as far as she could see, this was her only way of getting justice."

Samuel shifts in his seat, clears his throat. "I'm still a close friend of Heba's father, Mohammed," he says. "It's awful seeing him now – all the tragedy he's gone through has really knocked the life out of him, but he was a force to be reckoned with back in the day, especially during the First Intifada."

"I understand you were also a peace activist back then?" Hassan says. "Please, tell us about that."

"Okay," Samuel replies. "Let me begin by saying, like all Israelis I've done my time in the army. During my conscription, I fought in the Yom Kippur War, when Syria and Egypt attacked us, trying to claw back some of what was taken in the Six Day War of '67. I was in a tank in the Sinai Desert. I had friends in tanks on either side of me who lost their lives. When I returned from that war, I was more determined than ever to help Israel maintain its grip on the Palestinian territories, to keep us secure from future attacks. When my conscription was over, I opted to stay on as a reservist and over the many years that followed, I spent a lot of time in the West Bank.

"The Israeli army was as brutal then as it is today. We were issued billy clubs, and our standing orders were to "break arms and legs" of anyone posing a threat. The intention was to debilitate people, prevent them from causing trouble. Rabin was the Israeli Defence Minister at the time, and he issued the orders."

"The architect of the Oslo Accords!" says Hassan. "Clearly, he wasn't always so keen to talk peace!"

"Definitely not." Samuel shakes his head, pauses. "Unfortunately, the commander of my unit came from the same mould. He would keep petrol bombs, slingshots and knives in his jeep, ones he'd confiscated from Palestinians in the street, ready to use as justification if he was ever challenged by his superiors for any of the vicious things he did: ramming his vehicle into shop fronts or taking schoolkids off the street and holding them overnight. He never was challenged, of course, but he believed in being prepared.

"One day, we were out on patrol when we came across a blockade of old tyres, scrap metal and rubble dumped on the main road by Palestinian troublemakers trying to hinder us. My commander called over an old man from a nearby field and ordered him to clear it out of the way. He was going to stand back and watch the old guy struggle alone, so I went over to help him and my commander yelled at me, 'Come back, you idiot, there might be explosives in that pile!'. 'Then call the bomb squad!' I shouted back, and went ahead and helped clear the road.

"Another time, I was manning a security checkpoint when a car with Palestinian plates was stopped by my commander. The driver was explaining he had sick children in the back and he was heading to the clinic in the next town, and my commander was telling him that wouldn't be possible, he had to turn around and go back the way he'd come. Then my commander got a call on his walkie-talkie. From what I could hear, it was about his childminder not being able to pick up his daughter from school and he needed to arrange for someone else to do it. He was getting very hot under the collar, fretting that his daughter would be left standing at the school gates, while the car we'd stopped was still waiting there in the midday heat, the Palestinian father sat mute behind the wheel, the two sick children slumped in the back listless, their faces red with fever. It was such an obscene situation that I took matters into my own hands: I went up to the checkpoint, raised the barrier and cleared the car through. You see, I'd begun to resist where I could.

"The real change came when I was stationed in Hebron during the First Intifada back in '89 and met a remarkable young lady and her family. Out on patrol one day, we rounded up a bunch of kids, apparent troublemakers we found hanging around on the streets. When we got them back to the holding facility, one of these kids turned out to be a teenage girl, and since I was seen as the 'soft' one in the unit, I was ordered to guard her until she could be processed. We were waiting in the compound all afternoon, and got talking. She told me she'd run away from an Israeli employer on a nearby moshav who'd been treating her badly, making her work long hours without days off and withholding her pay when she'd complained. She was making her way home to her sister and brother-in-law when we'd picked her up. She said her family was like most Palestinians – all they wanted was to be left in peace to live their lives in their own land. I was surprised to hear this because I thought the general hope of Palestinians was to see Israel destroyed.

"I gave the girl a ride home that evening, after I'd finished duty and changed into civvies, and was invited in by her sister and her husband. We talked, and found we had something in common: we each believed in the 'two-state solution,' where an Israeli State and a Palestinian State could exist independently, side-by-side. They explained they threw rocks and burned tyres because how else could they protest the Occupation? I talked to them about the power of peaceful protest, and ways of doing that – marches, strikes, sit-ins, boycotts – and for a while, this is what they tried. One day, I was on duty when they marched through Hebron: men, women and kids chanting for the Israeli army to leave. I could see that my commander was readying to respond with tear gas and billy clubs, so I unloaded my gun, took off my army shirt, and went to stand with the protesters." Samuel grins ruefully. "My commander had me swiftly taken away and thrown in a cell for the night," he continues. "When I was released the next day and returned to duty, nothing more was said, but my commander had got the point. Next, my Hebron friends tried painting messages for peace on their houses, but Rabin soon issued an order banning all political slogans in public places in the West Bank, and the army painted over them. This was despite Israeli settlers continuing to scrawl their anti-Palestinian graffiti everywhere, of course.

"And then one day, the girl's brother-in-law was arrested by the army. He was taken away and locked in a cell, beaten and deprived of food, water and sanitation. He was interrogated about the source of funding for the intifada in Hebron, the role he was playing in it, and what was being planned next. On the day of his release, I drove to his house, eager to show my support, but he didn't ask me in. After that, he no longer hosted Israelis in his home and our activities came to a stop.

"But on the way home that day my car broke down just outside Beit Sahour, and that's when I met Mohammed, Heba's father. I wandered into his workshop looking for help, and he got me on my way again." Samuel shakes his head fondly at the memory. "He didn't care that I was Israeli – to him, I was simply someone who needed help. We became close after that, and went on to do some interesting things together in pursuit of peace."

The others around the table are looking at Samuel, waiting for more, but he suddenly feels drained by the memories. "I could carry on, tell you many more stories, but let's save that for another day," he says.

It's a good point to wind up the meeting, with everyone agreeing to get together again soon, and they spend the final few minutes batting around possible names for their group. Combatants No More? Unified Voices for Peace? Foes to Allies? They finally settle on Combatants United.

13

Reuben

Present Day – Millennium Arena, Tel Aviv

Reuben's life has taken a perverse turn since that terrible day he witnessed his daughter get caught in the radius of Heba's deadly payload. After that, he'd been forced to look at everything up close, to really question the cost of maintaining the bubble in which many Israelis live. For him, that bubble has been irretrievably pierced, burst into a million droplets and gone forever, leaving him with the dilemma of how to live in his exposed new world. But who'd have thought that Izzy's death would have sent him in this direction, working alongside Palestinians, the very people he had reason to hate? And that he'd be closest of all to Heba's father? They're partners in peace nowadays, Reuben and Mohammed, an unlikely duo given the connected circumstances of their daughters' deaths, but all the more powerful because of it. They go to schools in Israel and Palestine and talk to the kids, taking satisfaction in how their Palestinian-Israeli double act can disrupt the notion they're somehow different from each other, that they're from two opposing sides, and hopefully give the kids reason to think twice in their future encounters with *those others.* Besides the schools, they give talks to visiting international groups, they guide tours, they give interviews, always together, hoping their story will help open minds.

These memorial events are an annual check-up for Reuben, a chance to take an honest look in the mirror; to make sure he believes Mohammed's entitlement to pain is as legitimate as his own, and equally searing. He looks over at Mohammed and sees it there, in the lines of his face: the pain of his loss, not just of a daughter but of a granddaughter too. The two men are due up on stage soon, right after Caleb and Hassan, and he's concerned whether his friend is ready, composed after his late arrival. Mohammed looks okay, but he's trembling slightly with the strain of the evening and Reuben feels a swell of compassion for him. Maybe he should have gone to Beit Sahour to pick him up, brought him across the border himself and saved him from the additional stress? Damn, he just doesn't think sometimes! Before he'd arrived, Reuben had asked himself whether he could give the talk by himself. No, he couldn't. Having Mohammed by his side is the whole point. But his partner is here now and everything will be fine.

How differently it all could have turned out if he'd taken up his commander's offer for vengeance.

April 2007 – Revenge or Mercy?

There's someone at the door. They've got that no-nonsense knock of a person on a mission, nothing like the apologetic rat-a-tat-tat of the well-wishers. They never left them alone during those first few weeks after Izzy's death, the constant stream of visitors come to pay their respects. Her loss was public property back then, a cause for collective grief. Now, a year on, the visits are thinning out and they're left to themselves – his wife, their son and him – the grief theirs alone to work through. It's just the occasional phone call now, from a friend or neighbour checking to see how they're doing ("Okay, getting on with it, you know..."), asking if they're interested in coming around for dinner ("Thanks, maybe next month, when things get back to normal..."), or just to meet for coffee ("Sure, let's do that soon...").

There was one visitor in the early days who'd offered a very particular kind of condolence: revenge against the bomber's family. The visitor was the commander of Reuben's old army unit. He'd come during the seven-day mourning period to pay his respects and to brief Reuben on the investigation. Reuben had been desperate for information about his daughter's murder – he knew the bomber was a woman, he'd seen her with his own eyes, and he had a name, but who was she really, and why did she do it? Who helped her? Did her family and friends know what she was going to do? Part of him had thought having answers to these questions would help dissolve the pain; another part of him, the less emotional part, planned to store all the details away in a tightly sealed box until he was ready to do something with them.

"The bomber was from Beit Sahour, she worked for several years on-and-off as a chambermaid at the Tel Aviv Grand on the seafront," his commander had told him. "We've tracked down her parents and brother. They're all living together in a house on the outskirts of the village. The bomber was living alone, on the other side of the village."

"Isn't that unusual, a Palestinian woman living away from her family like that?" Reuben had said. "I wonder what that was about?"

"By the sound of things, she was a bit of a rebel," the commander had replied. "At one stage, she'd been married to a known troublemaker. He was shot at a checkpoint when he refused orders to get out of his car. Not that it's relevant, and it's nothing like what happened to Izzy, but we also found out this woman's daughter was killed during a flare-up between local Palestinian kids and the construction company working on the separation barrier in their village. She was hit in the back of the head by a rock thrown by one of the kids. The Palestinians claim the girl was shot by a soldier at the scene, but that's nonsense, of course. The Army's Chief of Staff personally led the enquiry into the incident and found it an open-and-shut case. We're working on the theory that's why she targeted him."

"And ended up killing a bunch of other people besides. These people just don't care, do they?" Reuben had said.

His commander had nodded in agreement. "Can you imagine, they even allow their own children to get in harm's way like that, with rocks flying about the place! This woman's daughter was only six years old. Our people did their best, rushed her to the hospital in West Jerusalem for treatment, operated on her, but she never recovered."

Reuben knew he should feel saddened by this young girl's death, but he had no room for anything but grief for his own loss. "That's terrible," he'd said, anyway.

"Don't feel too bad about it, Reuben. They brought it on themselves – they were the ones throwing the rocks. The point is, this woman murdered Izzy and her friends in cold blood. I promise you, the time will come very soon when we can have our revenge, and when that time comes, I will be back to get you."

Since those early days, Reuben has done all the things you'd expect of a grieving parent, but he's come to accept there's no instruction manual about how to get on with life after losing a child. There's a heavy, dark mass knotted up inside him, and he can't find an end to grab hold of, to begin to untangle it. There's been the funeral, and then the memorial organised by Izzy's school, but he'd sat numbly through both of those while beside him, his wife and son had quietly wept. Then there were the get-togethers with the other bereaved parents over cups of tea and photos, all of them in search of some relief through glimpsing the pain of the others. The girls, five of them, had their own rock band, Ruby Tuesday. Izzy had been the lead singer, and played guitar as well. Their last performance was on the school stage just a week before the bombing. Between them, the parents have had a recording studio built at the girls' school, a fitting memorial for their would-be rock stars. The other parents seem to be doing better, getting back to work, the gym, family days out. Even his wife is doing better than him. She's back in the office now, is managing to make conversation over dinner about her day, is making sure their son has clean clothes for school and does his homework, is keeping their fridge filled with all the right food. Reuben, on the other hand, is stuck. He has no appetite for the architecture practice he once loved, he can't make any plans or keep to a routine, the ins and outs of daily life are meaningless to him. He doesn't know, anymore, what he's here for.

He recently went along to a meeting of a newly formed group called Combatants United. From what he could gather about them, they were exactly what their name suggested: a bunch of Israelis and Palestinians who'd once fought on opposing sides of the Occupation, but who have now come together. To do what, precisely, he wasn't sure, and while the thought of meeting any Palestinian face-to-face was nauseating to him, he'd been told there'd be a man there who had some information about the bomber's family. As it happened, the information Samuel shared with him ended up turning Reuben's carefully guarded narrative about Heba and her kin on its head. Samuel told him about what happened after the publication of the army report on the killing of Heba's daughter, how he'd worked with an investigative journalist, also a member of Combatants United, and uncovered the truth that Jamila had been shot by an Israeli soldier, how they'd then failed to make the truth public, and how Heba had cut herself off after that. Reuben had been surprised to learn that Samuel was good friends with Heba's father, Mohammed, and his wife; that in his estimation they were a decent, ordinary family. They were struggling, too, Samuel said, grieving for their granddaughter and daughter, but also wracked with guilt for what their daughter had done and for their failure to stop it.

This wasn't what Reuben had expected to hear. He'd gone along to the meeting thinking he'd collect more ammunition to store away in his box of hate, waiting for the opportunity to open it up and put it all to use. What's he supposed to think now? Can he continue to believe the narrative of his commander, which would be so easy to do – that Izzy was another Israeli victim of an unprovoked and senseless Palestinian terrorist attack – or does he need to dig deeper, allow for the possibility, however difficult, that the bomber's actions were rooted in the kind of suffering he's going through himself, that her actions were the consequence of unrequited grief? And what about the bomber's parents: are they entitled to their grief, or should they be punished? He has a son to think about, Izzy's younger brother. One day, when he's eighteen, he'll be expected to serve his time in the army. What example should Reuben be setting for him? Revenge or mercy? Reuben still goes into Izzy's room every day and sits on her bed, trying to understand what she would have wanted him to do. If he can understand that, he knows he'll have his answer.

In recent years, before this happened to Izzy, he'd done his best to avoid the whole sordid business of the Occupation, to keep his family insulated from it. He'd been living in the Tel Aviv bubble, but he didn't care. He'd done his compulsory military service after high school and later, when the First Intifada came around and demanded more boots on the ground, he'd gone and done his part as a reservist. That was all they were getting from him. Back then, he was a newlywed and had his architect's practice to build, that was his focus. His wife worked with him in the business, keeping the books and handling the admin. Once the kids came along, Reuben's life was complete. He did his fair share of the school drop-offs and pick-ups, the after-school running around, the shopping and cooking, the bedtime reading. On any regular day, he was ready with the Dad jokes and tissues, depending on his offspring's needs. His home was filled with that elusive mix of wealth, health and happiness, and that was all that mattered.

When he'd seen Izzy and her friends on the street that day, he'd just finished a meeting with a group of developers working on the expansion of an Israeli settlement south of Hebron. They'd just confirmed his contract to design four blocks of apartments. They wanted them modern, bold, with plenty of mirrored glass and vertical gardens to offset the aridity of the surrounding area, and because they'd recently cleared extra land and caused a stir with the residents of some nearby caves, he'd need to incorporate good security features into his design: tempered glass, CCTV cameras, fireproof cladding, deep utility installations to keep the water and electricity supplies safe from interference. This was his first large-scale project, a big step up from the usual house extensions and shop fit-outs. Never mind its location, its colonial connotations – this was a huge opportunity for him. This was something to celebrate with the family later. With the extra cash, they'd be able to afford that holiday apartment in Eilat they wanted. That's where they'd spend their summers now, broaden their horizons, make new memories. When he'd seen Izzy coming down the street, he'd been excited to tell her all this. He'd shouted across to her and waved, started heading her way. And then the bomb exploded.

Reuben knows it's his commander at the door, from his no-nonsense knock, his promise last year that he'd be back when the opportunity for revenge presented itself. He goes to let him in, leads him through to the living room and offers him a seat. "Can I offer you a drink?" he asks. "Coffee, perhaps, or something stronger?"

"Thanks, Reuben, but I can't stay long. I wanted to tell you the Unit's been assigned to Beit Sahour, starting next month. It's the opportunity we've been waiting for. Join us as a reservist and we'll give that terrorist's family a little army treatment – get you the revenge you deserve."

Reuben is well aware what "a little army treatment" means, he's seen it first-hand during his duties. You barge through the front door of a Palestinian home, a group of five or more of you, shouting and pointing your rifles, going into every room and upturning furniture, smashing windows. You round up the family members in the living room, separating the women from the children, the men from the women, marching the men outside, bundling them into jeeps and carting them off for a few days' administrative detention, the women getting battered across the head with the butt of a rifle when they try to go to their kids to comfort them. He's seen the recent ones on the news, these "reprisal measures" carried out against the families of suicide bombers: bulldozers razing their homes to the ground, leaving them out on the street with nothing but the clothes they're wearing.

"I'll see you at the base next month, kitted up and ready for action," Reuben's commander says. "I've got your papers here." Reuben looks at the envelope his commander is offering him, but makes no move to take it. Should he? Revenge or mercy? It's time to decide. What would Izzy want him to do? What does her brother need from him? What about himself? Has he got it in him to wreak violence and sow hatred in the name of his sweet, loving girl?

"But how will that help, sir?" Reuben says. "The bomber's family isn't to blame for what she did. Harming them wouldn't be an act of revenge, it would serve only to stoke more fear and anger, lead to more violence." Reuben pushes the envelope away. "I must thank you, though, because you've helped me come to a decision."

That evening, Reuben sits down to write a letter to Heba's parents.

One year ago, we both lost our daughters, Izzy and Heba. I don't know if you saw the news from that day, but Izzy was one of the five schoolgirls who died. By a bizarre twist of fate, I was there when it happened and I saw it all. What can I tell you? One moment, Izzy was waving to me, happy and smiling, then she was looking at Heba and I think she saw what was about to happen because I could see fear on her face and she was about to scream or shout something, I don't know, and then there was the explosion. I could tell you what I saw in the aftermath as well, but no parent should have to hear about that. I would give anything to erase those images from my mind, but I think they'll be scorched there forever.

I've known for a while now that I need to do something exceptional to honour Izzy's memory, but it's been hard for me to figure out what that should be.

A few weeks back, I attended a meeting of Combatants United where I met a friend of yours, Samuel. He told me some great stories about what you all got up to in the '90s in the line of peaceful resistance – setting up the Palestinian-Israeli running club, and so on – and wow, all respect to you! He also told me about the tragedy your family has suffered since then and what Heba was trying to deal with. Samuel said enough for me to realise you are decent people – which was difficult, because I've mostly felt anger toward you and have wanted you punished. Then today, I got a visit from my old army commander, who offered me the chance of exactly that.

I chose not to accept my commander's invitation – I realised I can't let more blood be spilled, or suffering be caused, in my daughter's name. It's not what she would have wanted, and nor do I. Instead, I am writing this letter, the first step on a road to healing and finding some peace.

So, let me say this – with the background information I have, I don't blame anyone for what happened and I don't want revenge. No good can come from either of those. And I am ready to acknowledge your pain. If you feel able, I would like us to meet. By talking, I believe we can help each other heal.

I plan on giving this letter to Samuel to deliver to you. I hope one day to receive a reply. Until then, I wish you peace.

Yours,
Reuben Weiss

14

Mohammed

Present Day – Millennium Arena, Tel Aviv

Mohammed has come alone, which is usually the case these days. His wife has gone to their neighbours for the evening where they'll watch the ceremony on television. She prefers to stay close to home, but that doesn't mean she isn't supportive of what he's doing. His son, on the other hand, has no interest at all in Mohammed's activities with Combatants United and is probably up at the workshop this evening, keeping himself busy under the hood of a car. He says that since their family has lost so much to the Occupation, he wants nothing more to do with Israelis. He doesn't agree with his father's activities with Combatants United. He says he's working with the enemy and that they're normalising the Occupation. He says the Israelis should find their own peace first, clean up their own house. "We can talk when we're equal, not while they've got their boot on my neck," he says. Mohammed thinks differently, he believes in changing one mind at a time, that every Israeli who joins Combatants United, every youngster he manages to convince, is one less enemy to worry about.

On the stage, Caleb is talking about the importance of resolving the "Palestine Question" in the wake of the Abraham Accords. "It's a landmark step toward peace in the region to have Arab nations recognising the existence of Israel and, for the first time, welcoming Israelis into their countries for tourism and business," he says. "But the Palestinians can't be a thorn in everyone else's side while they move forward with this process. Palestinians need their own state, self-determination, to be left in peace. The time has come."

Good for Caleb for making the point, but Mohammed knows the reality they are facing: Palestinians are in a worse position today than they have been for decades. Back in 1989, Mohammed had believed it was just a case of reminding Israel that the Occupation was never meant to be permanent and it was time to leave, to get themselves back across the border. But like an invasive weed, they've penetrated further, planting their roots ever deeper with their multiplying settlements and military zones, making reversal nearly impossible.

He leans across to whisper in Samuel's ear. "Do you think things would have turned out differently if we'd been allowed to continue what we started in the First Intifada?" he asks.

1989 – The Wanted Eighteen

The people in Mohammed's village have had enough. They've just received their income tax bills from the Israeli government, and they're in no mood to pay. Why should they? What do they get in return? Military surveillance twenty-four hours a day, seven days a week, that's what they get. And another point: why should they be forced to buy their food, their utilities, their basics for living, from the Israelis? The Israelis control everything, demand payment, keep them poor. It's a "profitable occupation", that's for sure.

Yes, the inhabitants of Beit Sahour are ready to make a stand. A tax revolt, a push for economic independence, a show of non-violent civil resistance – they all agree this is what's required, but as they start out on this rebellious path, they're all over the place: some start growing their own vegetables, intending to boycott supplies coming from the nearby Israeli settlements; a few close up their shops to keep out the tax collectors; others fly Palestinian flags from their roofs and put up posters in their windows, "No Freedom, No Taxes", "Palestine Will Be Free"; and the kids take advantage of this general mood of insurrection by congregating on street corners, shouting and throwing stones at the army patrols when they pass through.

It's not long before the occupying regime begins its crackdown, trying to break the villagers' collective will by any means possible. Tax collectors start turning up at business premises and offering instant deals – pay a shekel and get the rest of your tax bill written off – tempting offers designed to undermine the tax revolt and put a dent in village unity. Curfews start getting imposed by the army, keeping everyone locked down in their homes often for days on end. Those caught in any act of rebellion get sentenced to "day prison", meaning they have to report to the nearby army base each day to sit idle in an empty room, waiting for the bell to ring, releasing them until the next day, when they have to come back and do nothing all over again. Schools get closed down, denying kids their education. The Palestinian flag gets banned, its right to exist also denied, and all those found flying in the village are confiscated. Army roadblocks are put up at the two main entrances to the village and vehicles are stopped, their occupants bullied for information on the activities of their neighbours.

The villagers can't carry on like this, obviously. They need to pull together and get themselves organised if they're going to succeed in their objectives. So, they set up a village committee in charge of overall strategy, and under this, sub-committees to handle various specific tasks: home schooling, tax withholding, food independence, curfew management, village morale. They even start a flag-making committee to defy the flag ban, setting up a makeshift production facility in one of the seamstresses' homes and buying the four different colours of fabric – red, green, black and white – from separate markets to avoid suspicion.

The sub-committee in charge of the tax revolt draws up general rules of engagement: all businesses should keep their doors open during normal trading hours and if the tax collectors turn up offering a "one shekel" deal, they should be refused. Well, this completely confounds the tax collectors, who then start showing up with soldiers in tow. They come to Mohammed's workshop one day, and when he turns down the "one shekel" deal, telling the tax collectors there's a principle at stake, they confiscate his tools. The same happens to the baker, the carpenter, and many others in the village. The tax men threaten to close down businesses, take away permits, seize houses. "Do whatever you want," is the villagers' unified response, "you can't force us to pay".

The sub-committee for village morale turns "day prison" into a community centre: the detainees sing and play instruments; they share their books, food and cigarettes;

they have lively debates about their situation over games of cards and backgammon. What can the army do about it? Either beat them or haul them off to a real prison, but they do neither. It's a calculated risk, and the villagers win.

And when curfews are imposed, the villagers are defiant. They congregate on their balconies, from where they cook food on their barbecues, play their music, drink arak, whisky and beer, converse with their neighbours through loudspeakers, wave their freshly made Palestinian flags at the infuriated soldiers patrolling the streets below and generally turn their lockdown time into a fiesta. The children are taught at home by their parents, and for the few hours that curfews are lifted, they're sent out around the village to distribute food and other supplies. In this way, the kids have no time for their rabble-rousing on street corners and everyone gets the supplies they need before the next lockdown begins.

Meanwhile, the sub-committee for food independence implements a collective model of production, getting each family in the village to grow crops in their back garden, or keep chickens for eggs, or goats for milk and meat. All the produce gets shared, distributed by the delivery boys and girls between curfews. Mohammed's family chooses to grow vegetables – potatoes, carrots and corn – composting the manure from next-door's goats to use as a highly effective fertilizer.

After a while, the sub-committee becomes more ambitious and decides to open a dairy farm, to enable the village to be self-sufficient in dairy products and boycott the milkman selling supplies from the nearby Israeli settlements. None of the villagers have any experience with cows. Sheep and goats, yes, but cows? Well, nobody has even met one before. With an unused workshop standing ready to be converted to a barn, it's decided that Mohammed is as good a choice as any to spearhead the dairy project and he launches into it with gusto. The fact he's never been within a hundred yards of a cow is not going to deter him.

But he soon hits upon the first problem – all cattle in the West Bank are owned by the moshavim and kibbutzim, the Israeli agricultural settlements. If the village wants cows, it's going to have to go against its new-found revolutionary conscience and buy them from the Israeli farmers; and presumably, the Israelis, too, won't be easily convinced to sell their cows to their Palestinian customers. Mohammed will need to formulate a plan.

Earlier that year, Mohammed had helped an Israeli who'd broken down on the road outside the village and walked into his workshop seeking help. He seemed a nice enough man, and Mohammed wasn't one to turn away someone in need, so he'd taken him in his tow truck back to his car, identified the problem as a broken fan belt, replaced it and got him on his way. The man's name was Samuel. He'd told Mohammed he owed him one, and if ever he could return the favour, he should give him a call. So Mohammed does just that. He calls Samuel and asks if he can help the villagers procure a dozen or so cows from one of the settlements in the area. Samuel says he'll see what he can do, that he'll make a few calls. A week goes by, and Mohammed hears nothing, but then one morning Samuel gets in touch. "I think I've managed to find you eighteen cows," he says. "An old army friend runs a dairy farm in Moshav Patza'el. He's heard about what you're trying to do in Beit Sahour and he's sympathetic to the cause." Samuel goes on to explain that this farmer is one of the few peacenik

Zionists in the West Bank, he wants everyone to be equal, Israelis and Palestinians alike. He can spare eighteen cows for their cause, but he'd like twelve goats and three dozen chickens in return. Mohammed agrees immediately, and they arrange to meet at the moshav the next day. Within twenty-four hours of receiving Samuel's call, Mohammed has procured the necessary number of chickens and goats from his bemused neighbours and borrowed a lorry from a construction company in Bethlehem to transport the loads. Thus prepared, he and his two kids, Heba and Mohammed Jr., set off eagerly for the moshav to meet Samuel and his farmer friend and complete the animal exchange.

The goats and chickens are offloaded from the lorry by the farmer's two Palestinian helpers. Mohammed knows that Palestinians in the rural villages struggle to make a living under the Occupation, and if it's a choice between seeing their families starve or working for the Israelis, they'll often work for the Israelis. Boycotting isn't an option for these people and they don't deserve his judgment. At least these two seem to be working for one of the decent ones. Mohammed chats with them as they check over the goats and chickens, and listens when they tell him the cows he's getting in exchange are prime stock, the best milk producers around, but that he'll need to get himself a bull, too, if he wants that to continue. He raises the question with the farmer, who tells him that once he's got the cows settled in, to come back with more goats and chickens and he'll trade them for a sire.

The farmer and his farmhands deftly herd the eighteen cows into the back of Mohammed's borrowed lorry, one behind another in a neat and obedient line, and Mohammed begins the ten-kilometre drive back to Beit Sahour. He and the two kids are completely delighted with their load and are feeling very pleased with themselves, until the skies cloud over and the rain starts to pour, darkening the afternoon around them and dampening their spirits. The dirt roads become slick with mud, and Mohammed is forced to slow to a crawl as the lorry begins to slip and slide. He tries to avoid the crevices and rocks, mindful of the mooing load in the back. Slowly but surely, they reach the crossroads at the edge of the village, a point in the road where it starts to climb steeply upward, and it's here they realise the cows' journey, and their task, is far from over, because Mohammed's workshop, the cows' new home, is at the top of that hill. He shifts the lorry into low gear, firmly grips the steering wheel and puts his foot down steady on the accelerator, letting out the clutch slowly until he feels the gears bite and the wheels start to turn, and turn, and turn... going nowhere. There's too much rainwater gushing down the road, bringing with it a year's worth of accumulated sand and dirt turned to mud, and they can't get any traction. "It's no good," he tells Heba and Mohammed Jr. "We'll have to offload the cows here and walk them up the hill."

Volunteers are needed. They leave the lorry and dash through the rain in three different directions, knocking on doors to round up their neighbours. A small crowd soon gathers around the lorry. A handful of men have agreed to help herd, while the women and kids gather to watch. This is a new experience for everyone and there's excitement in the air, despite the stormy conditions. Mohammed lets down the tailgate and waits for the cows to walk themselves down the ramp. They don't move. So, Mohammed jumps into the lorry and starts to push them from behind. This is greeted with lots of shifting around and mooing, but no forward progress toward the ramp.

They were happy enough to be loaded onto the lorry back at the moshav, Mohammed thinks. *Why wouldn't they be just as happy to get out again?* And then he remembers: the farmhands back at the moshav were using cattle prods and hay to get them loaded, their "stick and carrot approach", as they called it. *Of course, that's what we need to do!* Mohammed sends a bunch of the kids up the hill to his workshop to bring down a bale of hay, and he sends other kids to their houses to fetch brooms. Now four of the men grab the brooms, jump onto the lorry and push their way through the cows to the back, while others start throwing armfuls of hay onto the ramp, trying to entice the cows out. It begins to work. Slowly, slowly, the cows begin to move, following the hay trail down the ramp and onto the road. And then it all goes terribly wrong. Rather than stand in an orderly herd awaiting further instructions, the cows keep on walking, down the road and back in the direction they've just come from. Mohammed and the other men have to rush to stop them and try to turn them around. This is when the cows get confused and panicky and begin lumbering off in all directions.

Well, the village has its very own version of the "Running of the Bulls" that night, as eighteen bellowing cows run amok through the streets, chased down by the men, hollering and wielding brooms and armfuls of hay, pursued by the children, whooping and shrieking, and their distraught mothers running along behind them, imploring them to "stop!" and "come back!" It's a couple of crazy hours before they manage to round those cows up and get them to the top of the hill and into Mohammed's workshop. There they stand placidly, chomping on hay and letting off steam from their rain-soaked hides. The villagers crowd around them watching, exhausted, wet and dirty, but completely enchanted.

And so, on what becomes one of the most oft-recounted nights in village history, the eighteen cows are adopted into Beit Sahour daily life. Everyone is enthralled by them and they receive a constant stream of visitors, dawn through to dusk. When, about a month after their arrival, one of the cows gives birth, it's to a delighted crowd cramming into the former workshop to welcome their new addition. And when autumn arrives and the evenings start to turn cold, the cows start receiving night-time visitors too: after Heba's chance meeting with one of them, a gang of teenage boys from the nearby refugee camp wanted by the Israeli army for their "terrorist activities" and therefore unable to go home to their own beds at night, choose instead to nestle down in Mohammed's barn, taking advantage of the warmth of the cows and the softness of the hay bales. Mohammed doesn't often see these visitors, they're almost always gone by the time he and his kids get there in the mornings, but sometimes they're still around and he gives them milk and eggs, telling them to go home and see their families.

It's not long before the army hears about the cows and the villagers have to implement a plan to keep them safe from prowling soldiers. The teenagers are swiftly assigned to this important operation. It becomes their job to alert the village when the army patrols turn up, sounding the alarm with a chain of bird calls from one street to the next, until the message reaches Mohammed, who quickly turns off the workshop lights, closes and shutters the windows and bolts the doors, keeping the cows safely hidden inside.

One day, however, the military governor comes striding into Mohammed's workshop flanked by a dozen soldiers who quickly get busy photographing each cow, taking their headshots and the unique numbers branded on their rumps. The governor tells Mohammed he has to get rid of the cows, either return them to where they came from or slaughter them. When Mohammed asks why, the governor angrily replies, "Because they're a threat to the security of the State of Israel!"

Mohammed has never heard anything so ridiculous. A threat to the Israeli dairy industry, maybe – but a security threat? "But how?" he asks, genuinely perplexed.

"You are not permitted to ask questions!" the governor snaps. "This is a military order. If you disobey it, you will be jailed."

Mohammed is given twenty-four hours to close the dairy, or else it will be bulldozed to the ground. With their independent milk supply under threat, it's time once again for the villagers to swing into action. The butcher kindly agrees to take the cows and he hides them in his slaughterhouse, so when the governor comes back to Mohammed's workshop the next day, he finds it empty. He asks Mohammed where they are, and Mohammed looks him in the eye and replies, "Gone, as you ordered." The governor holds his stare for a moment or two longer than Mohammed finds comfortable, but then he pulls his Ray-Bans back down over his eyes, turns on his heels and marches out of the workshop, his dozen soldiers trotting to keep up.

The village's independent milk production has survived another day, continuing to operate from its new location, and the kids on the dairy delivery team carry on hauling it around the village by carts and wheelbarrows, filling pots and pans left ready on doorsteps.

Of course, it's not long before the army again twigs that the eighteen cows are still around and keeping the villagers supplied with fresh milk. After all, the regular Israeli milkman hasn't seen any resumption in business since the governor closed the Beit Sahour dairy. It's no surprise, then, when one day, as dusk is falling, a siren sounds through the village and an open-top army jeep passes through, informing the villagers by loudspeaker that a curfew is being imposed "until further notice". This time the curfew lasts all night and day, so the kids can't get out to distribute the milk. Instead the doctor, still permitted to visit his patients, offers to become the delivery man, transporting buckets of milk in the back of his car.

Determined not to be thwarted once again, the army proceeds to mount a comprehensive search and seizure operation. "Produce the cows and you will be freed from your homes," the patrolling jeeps intone as helicopters circle overhead. Dozens of soldiers take part in the operation, swarming through the village like ants and knocking on every door. "Have you seen these cows?" they demand, waving photos of the cows and their numbered rumps at surprised residents. The search continues for three straight days, before the army eventually tracks the herd down to the slaughterhouse. The military governor comes back and informs the butcher the cows are to be confiscated.

"You can't do that," the butcher tells him. "We got these cows from an Israeli farmer in an honest deal, and now you want to confiscate them? You must pay us for them, or we are not letting you have them. It's our right, we have a butcher's shop, and these cows are to be slaughtered and their meat sold. You have a problem with that?"

But it does no good. The governor barks his orders and the soldiers haul the butcher off to detention and take the cows away in a flat-bed truck, never to be seen by the villagers again.

Time goes by and, like other communities throughout the West Bank, the villagers of Beit Sahour keep up their efforts to resist the Occupation. After Samuel's help with procuring the cows, Mohammed has stayed in touch with him and they've become good friends. They decide to start a running club together, Runners for Peace, with a mixed membership of Palestinians and Israelis, meeting up once a week to run through the streets of Beit Sahour. Soon, they get ambitious and organise a half-marathon, with all the runners wearing the same T-shirts: "We want peace between Israel and Palestine" emblazoned across their fronts, and "Each free and secure" on their backs. But the army commander orders the arrest of the Israeli journalists covering the event, and makes the runners turn their T-shirts inside out and walk back to the starting point, shepherded by army jeeps. Not to be defeated, Samuel and Mohammed organise a re-run of the event a few weeks later, this time getting sponsorship from *Runners World*. With its global circulation, coverage by a magazine like this means the eyes of the world are on them, which is excellent, not only because it helps spread their call for peace, but also because it means the army doesn't dare interfere. This time around, over two hundred runners get to finish the race, and a photo of the winners, sloganized T-shirts and all, makes the cover of the next *Runners World*.

Emboldened by the success of the half-marathon, Mohammed and Samuel start organising other joint Israeli-Palestinian activities in the village. They make signs for the residents to hang on the outside of their houses: "We want peace between a Free Palestine and a Secure Israel" and "Break Bread, Not Bones". Samuel and other Israelis bring their families for the weekends, staying in Palestinian homes, partying in the square with music and dancing, encouraging their children to play together.

The problem, however, is that not all sections of Palestinian society are as peaceful in their resistance. The First Intifada becomes increasingly violent, and by the early '90s international pressure is being brought to bear on the Palestinian leadership to scale back the violence and come to the negotiation table. The Oslo Accords is the result. The inhabitants of Beit Sahour feel deflated: they have dreamed of so much more than this. They strongly believe that their central leadership has given in too early, that through their own actions, and the pressure of the intifada, they are close to achieving nationhood, independence, freedom, if they can push on for just a while longer. But, alas, the Palestinian Authority has made its decision and the villagers are instructed to wind down their activities. Many Palestinians celebrate the Accords, believing the process will eventually lead to peace – they put roses in the guns of the patrolling soldiers and they sing and dance in the streets – but for Mohammed and his neighbours it's a profound let down.

It's 1995 by now, and Mohammed's kids are no longer kids. His son has chosen to follow in his footsteps and works with him in his workshop. Heba, on the other hand, is eager to get out into the world after so many years of lockdown, and with Samuel's help, she's got herself a job in a Tel Aviv hotel. Mohammed consoles himself with the thought that they're tourist dollars paying her wages, dollars that would otherwise find their way into the pockets of her Israeli counterparts. When she tells him one day she's going to the Kings of Israel Square to celebrate the Accords alongside Israelis, and he sees her so full of excitement and hope, Mohammed doesn't have the heart to dissuade her. *Let her have her moment,* he thinks, *she's made sacrifices too, missing her education, running chores around the village when she should have been playing. It's up to her, now; let her have her freedom.* And so Heba goes to the Square to celebrate and she's ready, completely, to embrace the opportunity of living her life side by side with Israelis. But then the political process that Oslo kickstarted fizzles to nothing, its death confirmed at Camp David in 2000, bringing in its wake the Second Intifada, this one more violent than the first. There's the Wall, the roadblocks, the soldiers who kill Tariq and Jamila. The notion of Israelis being her friends becomes a cruel joke that ultimately backfires, ending the lives of several of them along with her own.

April 2007 – A Surprise Visit

Since Heba's death, Mohammed has withdrawn from the world. He feels guilty he wasn't able to stop her, he feels ashamed at what she did, he feels weighed down by the loss – Heba gone so soon after Jamila and Tariq. There's a feeling of hopelessness, too, because everything he and others around him had worked for during the First Intifada has brought them to this place, which is far worse than before. Despite what Samuel might say, he still believes their friendship, born from that place of peace, has come under strain through Heba's actions. Their children used to play together, for goodness sake. Will he ever feel he genuinely has Samuel's kinship again? His wife is dealing with it all in her own way, holding nightly vigils in their living room when neighbours come around and they mourn together, not just for Heba, Jamila and Tariq, but for everyone they have lost in the violence. Mohammed Jr. has become a workaholic as his way of dealing with things, seven days a week, twelve hours a day in the workshop, but that's also a matter of necessity now that Mohammed no longer shares the load.

Apart from the neighbours calling on his wife, the last visitor to the house was Samuel who'd come to tell him about a new group they were forming: Combatants United. Eva was involved, too, along with some Palestinians from Aida, the refugee camp. Samuel thought it would be good for Mohammed to come along to the meetings, see how it went. His friend reminded him of everything they'd achieved together during the First Intifada: procuring the eighteen cows from the moshav, their running club, the sleepovers. He also reminded him that he himself had also failed Heba when he couldn't get the truth out about Jamila's death, denying her the redress she so desperately needed.

But Mohammed wasn't interested – activism had failed. "What's the point?" he told Samuel. "Where did it get us last time? We tried to build bridges, but we got walls. Palestine's hope was my hope, now there's just sorrow."

That was a few months back and now people leave him alone to be with his thoughts. He's rallying himself to go into the kitchen and put the kettle on when a loud knock on the door startles him and he falls back into the chair. It's a purposeful knock, official sounding, not the almost-apologetic rap of the neighbours calling on his wife. Mohammed has been fearing this, a visit from the army, the reprisal attack for what Heba has done. At least no one else is at home; it's only him they can get. If they are going to do it, then it should be now.

He listens intently for the tell-tale sounds of hissed commands, shuffling boots, the clicking of firearms being readied, but he can't hear anything above the tick-tocking of the clock in the hallway. He sits and waits, his back tense, his heart thumping, his ears straining. Is that voices he can hear? And then comes the sound of a key unlocking the front door – the soldiers are letting themselves in!

"Mohammed, I'm home! And look who I found on the doorstep!"

His wife comes bustling into the living room with Samuel in tow. Mohammed is faint with relief, but the two of them are oblivious – she's taking off her coat and heading into the kitchen, and their guest is making himself comfortable on the sofa.

"It's okay, I haven't come to talk you into joining our peace organisation again," Samuel assures. "I've come to give you this." He produces an envelope from his coat pocket and offers it to Mohammed. "I should warn you before you open it, it's from the father of one of the schoolgirls killed in Heba's bombing last year."

Mohammed sinks back into his chair, fearful to take the letter as if it, too, might detonate in his hands. With this envelope, Samuel has brought the world back into his house, demanding to be faced. He's not about to say "thank you".

"His name is Reuben," Samuel explains. "He came to one of our Combatants United meetings last year, a few weeks after the bombing. I guess we didn't provide the answers he was looking for, because we didn't see him again, and then yesterday he contacted me to ask that I deliver this letter to you. For what it's worth, I believe its contents are conciliatory. Go on, take it."

Mohammed takes the envelope and opens it. He takes out the letter, a single sheet filled with neat, spiky handwriting in purple-blue ink. "Nice paper," he says, and starts to read.

15

Omar

Omar is riveted by Caleb's speech. "Let's make the decision to live side by side in peace and not let our differences be the cause for conflict any longer," he's saying. "It's true that Israelis and Palestinians have different cultures, religions, languages, histories – we should accept those differences, respect them, celebrate them. After all, what a boring world this would be without them. But do any of those differences mean that one group has a stronger right to survive than the other...?"

That's the guy who shot me, Omar thinks. *He's up there talking peace and understanding because of me; everything he's done with his life since he shot me, he's done because of me. Does that make my shooting worth it, was that the reason for it? If Caleb shooting me sent him running towards peace, but me down the path of violence, do they cancel each other out?* Omar knows he can make this a two-nil score in peace's favour. He also knows it's within his power to give Caleb that one thing no other person, and none of his fervent activities, can: forgiveness.

June 2015 – Prison, the Revolutionary University

Omar is eight years into a twelve-year prison sentence. He shares a cell with fellow "terrorists" or "political prisoners", depending on whom you ask – eighteen of them in all, crammed into a cell the size of a cargo container. The prison has a dozen of these cells in total, each with a bucket for a toilet, dank foam mats to sit and sleep on, scratchy, fetid blankets for bedding and nothing else. Prisons like this are in the business of breaking spirits. The Israeli guards are specially trained in it, and have an array of tactics at their disposal, physical as well as psychological. Prodding, slapping and verbal abuse are the norm and, for the particularly unruly, there are cold showers, solitary confinement, confiscation of clothing, withholding of meals, turning away of family and friends on visiting days. The list goes on.

Over time, the prisoners have developed their own tactics to defend themselves against these harsh conditions, to stay strong and united. They've implemented a system to govern themselves by, good enough to rival any village council, and it's a democratic one, too, because they've arranged themselves along political lines: Fatah, Hamas, Third Way, Popular Front – everyone's a member of one of them, and they each hold regular meetings and participate in cross-party debates to keep their ideologies alive. There's a multi-partisan system of committees, too: the education committee hosts lectures and film nights on topics from beekeeping to the Second World War; the entertainment committee keeps spirits high with regular offerings of music and plays; and the welfare committee devises ways to fight for improved prison conditions. All positions are filled and all decisions are made through voting, done behind their guards' backs, because democracy in prison is apparently a crime. And the committees keep their agendas full: the prisoners watch *Schindler's List* and *The Book Thief* to learn the history of their adversaries, to try to understand them; they've composed their own anthem to sing each night at lights-out time, *You can imprison our bodies but not our souls*; and they go on hunger strike, often for ten days or more in a row, taking only salty water to sustain themselves by while lobbying for better food, bedding, sanitary conditions, more time in the yard.

To spread awareness of these strikes and to garner support, the prisoners scrawl messages on toilet paper, wrap them in plastic, and get them transported out of prison in their visitors' mouths, to be swallowed in the event of search, but otherwise destined for the students' union at the nearby university and to other prisons in the area. The guards do their best to break these hunger strikes. They cook their own food on barbecue grills in the yard, wafting the tantalising aromas through the barred windows and into the cells where the prisoners lie listless. Prisoners' families are told they're close to death in the hopes they'll coax them into eating again. Ring-leaders get transferred to other prisons.

"Welcome to the Revolutionary University!" Omar's fellow inmates had greeted him with on his first day, and they weren't wrong. This is fertile ground for the mind, and he's getting himself an education. He's got a job in the prison library and has taken to reading, working his way slowly through all the books, staying awake long into the night to read the likes of Martin Luther King's *Strength to Love*, Gandhi's *Experiments with Truth*, even Frank's *Diary of a Young Girl*. He's never really read books before, but if he had, it wouldn't have been these. He'd be more of a sci-fi person, given the choice, but whoever runs the prisons clearly has other ideas. He's learning from these books, though, and beginning to look at things in a different way. He's willing to see where all this will take him. After all, nothing he's done with his life so far has worked out too well – just look where he is.

There's nobody more surprised than him that one of the people he's closest to in here is an Israeli prison guard. It was one night about three years ago, way after lights-out time, and everyone else in Omar's cell was sprawled across the floor, fast asleep on their mats. Omar was feeling restless and was standing at the front of the cell, reading by the green haze of the night light in the corridor. He was holding the book through the bars, trying to angle the scant light onto the page, when Samuel came through on his rounds. "What have you got there?" he asked, aiming his torch at the book.

Omar quickly pulled it back through the bars, as if caught red-handed with something illicit. "It's just a book," he said.

Samuel chuckled. "I can see that! I mean, which one is it?"

Omar held the book up and showed Samuel the cover. "It's the one about Nelson Mandela. *Long Walk to Freedom*."

"Great book," Samuel said. "Where are you in the story?"

"He's just left boarding school."

"You've got quite a way to go," Samuel replied, and passed his torch through the bars. "You'll need this if you want to finish the book before you get out of here."

That torch was one of the most valuable gifts Omar had ever received. Plus the batteries, of course, which Samuel continued to keep him supplied with over the years that followed. They had regular discussions after that, the two of them standing either side of the bars, their faces made ghostly in the green gloom. Samuel told him all about his activities during the First Intifada, what he and his friend Mohammed got up to in their pursuit of non-violent resistance to the Occupation – the stories of the dairy farm, their sleepovers, the running group they put together. "It's all about the power of peaceful resistance," he explained to Omar. "Like Mandela, Gandhi, Dr. King."

When Omar asked Samuel how, if he was so against the Occupation, he'd managed to serve in the Israeli army, and was now a prison guard, when both roles were so oppressive to Palestinians, Samuel replied he'd treated his army days as a chance to "influence from within", to set an example to his comrades about how the people who were subjected to the Occupation ought to be treated. He'd chosen to go into the prison service for the same reasons, to encourage his colleagues to treat prisoners with respect, as human beings, but also, because he wanted to maintain his contact with Palestinians at the forefront of the Occupation, to talk with them about solutions. He was a founding member of Combatants United, he told Omar, a joint Israeli-Palestinian organisation focused on resisting the Occupation through non-violent means.

One day, Samuel asked Omar what he'd done to earn a twelve-year prison sentence. Omar gave him the short, brutal version, aiming to shock this guy, to test his fancy ideas about peace. He told Samuel he'd been picked up at the Wall carrying an incendiary device he proposed to plant under the car of one of the "suits" working on the expansion of the Israeli settlement near his home. That was Omar's mission back then, he told Samuel: to resist to exist by force as necessary. He was on a borrowed scooter and he'd followed the "suit" from the settlement, waiting for him to make a stop and present the opportunity to strike, but the guy had driven straight to the border gates at the Wall and crossed through into Israel, and Omar's chance had slipped away. He'd made a note of the registration number of the guy's vehicle, planning to add it to the list of all the other officials he'd identified working at the settlement. He would try again, and next time he wouldn't fail. But there never was a next time because Omar had been stopped and searched that first time, and here he was. "Whoever that guy was, he was lucky," Omar told Samuel.

"When was this?" Samuel asked.

"Eight years ago. Why?"

"It could have been Reuben you were following."

Omar frowned. "I didn't know any of the targets' names, only their vehicle details," he said. "Who's Reuben?"

"He's an architect I know who was working on the expansion of the settlement above Khaybar Caves, but he withdrew from the project in 2007, just before he joined Combatants United."

Samuel went on to tell Omar about the death of Reuben's daughter, Izzy, from a suicide bombing in Tel Aviv and how, when Reuben had found out more about this bomber and what had happened to her husband and daughter, he had rejected a chance for revenge against the bomber's family and had instead become a peace activist. Part of that was withdrawing from the settlement project, handing it over to another architect. "Nowadays, he's helping to rebuild

Palestinian homes damaged by settlers or torn down by the Israeli army," Samuel explained. Another important step Reuben took was contacting the woman's family to tell them he understood. "I was the middleman, carrying letters between them, because I knew the family well," Samuel said. "It was Mohammed, the friend I've told you so much about – it was his daughter who killed Izzy. Mohammed and Reuben now work together to prevent what happened to their two daughters from ever happening again."

Omar stood quiet for a moment when he heard this. "If it was Reuben I followed that day, then I'm glad I failed," he said. "The poor guy wouldn't have deserved the ending I had planned for him."

"But that's the point, isn't it?" Samuel said. "Are we sure anybody actually deserves the violence we inflict on each other? Do we have the right to make that judgment?"

Over time, as trust between the two men grew, Omar told Samuel more of his own story. After recovering from gunshot wounds he'd sustained at the hands of the Israeli army, he'd become a policeman, a member of the Palestinian Civil Police Force, he told him, but then his friend Khaled had been killed by an Israeli soldier a stone's throw from where he was standing in uniform. "Khaled was the finest, most gentle human being you could hope to meet. The day I was injured, he was the one who stopped the bleeding and rushed me to hospital. I owed my life to Khaled, and after they killed him, I vowed to get revenge. I went underground, joined the Marzen militia. I took part in armed attacks against Israeli army posts and settlements all over the West Bank, but my special target was the settlement above Khaybar – I had to stop its expansion, and I wanted to destroy it." He told Samuel how he'd worked with a couple of other Marzen members, ransacking building supplies, stealing tools, damaging the contractor's vehicles, and generally making life as difficult as possible. They had the senior officials in their sights, too, shadowing them, threatening them, doing whatever it took to deter them from the project. "Hence my targeting of your friend, Reuben, or whoever it was that day."

When Samuel asked Omar about the day he'd been wounded, Omar told him it was something they experienced all too often at Khaybar, "getting attacked by our friendly neighbours from the Israeli settlement on the hill, the army rushing to their aid when we tried to defend ourselves with whatever we could find, getting fired at and left for dead. Can you believe, the soldier who shot me came back six months later wanting to apologise! He's lucky I wasn't there to hear his pathetic explanations!"

"I know this story," Samuel said, shocked. "I know the soldier who fired at you – his name is Caleb. He's a refusenik now, because of you. And he's a founding member of Combatants United."

"That's great, but it's not enough for me to forgive him," Omar replied. "My mother still has the letter he left for me. I can't bring myself to open it, to give him the satisfaction."

Omar and Samuel's nightly discussions are now drawing to a close, because Samuel is finally retiring and hanging up his prison guard's uniform for good. He's come to say goodbye, bringing with him a farewell gift: a new torch and enough batteries to see Omar through the next four years. "Keep up the reading," he tells Omar, shaking his hand. "I'll be waiting for you when you get out, and then you must come along to one of our meetings, finally meet the guy who derailed you."

"We'll see," Omar replies. "That day is still a long way off."

16

Caleb

Of all the thousands of people in the audience listening to his speech, there's one particular person Caleb's eager to reach: Omar.

It's been three years since Omar first turned up at a Combatants United meeting, and still they haven't spoken. Caleb's looking in Omar's direction, fixing his gaze just above the guy's head and willing him to listen as he tells the audience that he devotes all his free time to the cause nowadays, that he spends his weekends in the West Bank countryside with Combatants United, supporting the villagers against settler incursions and army bullying. They've had tear gas and live fire used against them, they've been thrown to the ground, hospitalised, handcuffed and taken away. "The *World's Most Moral Army* in action! What a disgrace!" Caleb says. "If this is how Israel's army treats its own citizens who stand up for the human rights of our neighbours, just think how the army treats those neighbours, the Palestinians who live under its Occupation."

July 2015 – Visiting Rumaya

Hassan called Caleb and the others early this morning, telling them they were needed in Rumaya, a village in the far north of the West Bank. And here they all are, bumping their way there aboard the Combatants United minibus.

Hassan uses the journey to brief everyone on the situation. A few hours ago, just before dawn, he tells them, one of the houses on the outskirts of Rumaya was firebombed. The house belongs to a family Hassan knows. The front door was kicked in, the ground floor windows were smashed, and petrol bombs were thrown inside. Within minutes, the whole house was ablaze. Israelis from the nearby settlement are the suspected culprits. They've been bothering this family for years, accusing them of "harbouring terrorists", when in fact all they've been doing is helping Palestinian lads released from the nearby prison to find their way home. Tensions have been running particularly high recently after a pet dog belonging to one of the settlers was bashed over the head with a rock and left dead in a nearby field. The settlers have been bent on revenge, and not interested in hearing that it was an act of self-defence, that the poor lad who'd been viciously attacked by said "pet" dog was a bleeding, sobbing mess when they'd found him, that his face had needed to be put back together with reconstructive surgery and extensive stitching.

"And now an eighteen-month-old girl has been burned to death, along with her mother and father," Hassan says. "The grandparents managed to get out, along with their four-year-old grandson. They've been taken to a hospital in Israel – they're all badly burned and in critical condition. The funerals for the toddler and her parents are taking place this afternoon, and the whole village will be joining the funeral procession. Afterward, there will be a vigil in the field across from the house to pray for the recovery of the rest of the family. Settlers are likely to be there, agitating from the sidelines, stoking tensions, and the army has been called in "to keep the peace". We're going there to support the villagers, to keep them safe while they do what they need to do." Hassan looks at Caleb and the other Israelis on the bus: Reuben, Samuel and Eva. "Your presence today will be a big help – the settlers and army will toe the line when they know there are Israeli peace activists in attendance, keeping an eye on things."

"How do you know the family?" Caleb asks. "The village is a long way from where you live."

"You remember I told you about my brother being shot in '89 by that soldier, Ice? After that, my mother wanted me to quit the gang I was in and stay out of trouble, she didn't want another son killed, and she needed me at home. So I promised her I would give it up, and I moved back home and got a job on a construction site. I was working during the day and coming home to sleep at night. She was happy. But then one day, on my way back from work, I was stopped in the street by an army patrol. Soldiers jumped out of the back of the jeep and surrounded me. Then that bastard Ice opens the passenger door and steps down, and he's sneering like a lunatic. He comes right up to me, and he's got his face right in mine and he's staring at me, still with that horrible sneer. "You got any more brothers I should know about?" he says. Well, I saw red at that, went to throw a punch, but I got restrained by the soldiers and next thing I know, I'm being manhandled into the back of the jeep and hauled off to detention.

"I was given a six-month sentence, and because of my age – fifteen – they sent me to juvenile prison. It was horrible. Bad food, bad sanitary conditions, grey concrete cell blocks, really basic. But what I remember most is how freezing it was the whole time. It was winter, and we were up here in the north where it's much colder. There was no source of heat in the prison, only a thin blanket to keep you warm. Farm animals get treated better. And because I was so far from home, it was difficult for anyone to come and visit. My mother came once, a journey that took three buses, five hours each way. She wasn't pleased about it, I can tell you." Hassan chuckles at the memory. "When she got there, they only let her stay for ten minutes and she spent the whole time giving me an earful for providing the army an excuse to haul me off.

"I made friends with the guy in the next cell, and we traded stories about our worst run-ins with the Israeli army. He was from Hebron, the old historic part where Israeli settlers live above the Palestinians and throw their rubbish down on top of them. There are nets strung up across the alleyways to catch the worst of it, but still, it sounded very unpleasant. I told him I wanted to see it for myself one day, and we planned for me to visit when we were both out. As it happened, he got released two nights before me.

"When it was my turn for release, it was the same as for everyone else: no prior notice and done in the middle of the night. They just grabbed me from my cell, walked me out through the front gate and left me standing there, out in the cold. I still had my blanket wrapped around me, thank goodness, but I had no food or water, no money and no clue where I was. I walked down the road and just kept going straight, for what felt like hours. I eventually came to a village, but couldn't knock on any of the doors because I didn't know who was inside. It was still dark, but from what I could make out the houses looked Palestinian, old and constructed of stone, not modern like the Israeli settlements, but who knew in that part of the country? I'd never seen any of it before.

"I learned from the road sign that the village was called Rumaya. I decided to wait until it was light and people were out and about, then I'd get a better idea of who they were. I hunkered down in a ditch at the side of the road, trying to keep warm and out of sight. There was a row of houses across from where I was hiding and I watched the lights come on behind curtains as people started to wake up. Around dawn, a front door opened and a boy came out. He was my age, maybe a little older – seventeen or eighteen, perhaps. From his features and the way he was dressed – old jeans, scruffy, baggy sweatshirt – I thought he was probably Palestinian, but then I heard a woman shouting after him, telling him to put his coat on, and I knew I was on safe ground – they were Palestinian, definitely. So I went up to the front door and knocked. No answer. I knocked again, harder this time, and a man came to the door. The boy's father, I assumed, because they looked alike: tall, thin, curly black hair. But the guy looked stern, like he wasn't pleased to see me.

"'I've just been released from the prison,' I told him, and pointed down the road in the direction I'd walked from. When he heard this, the guy's features softened. He pulled me into the house and quickly shut the door behind me. "Come in, young man. You're safe here," he said, and I instinctively knew that I was. He sat me down at the kitchen table and gave me coffee and a plate of eggs, falafels and flatbread. His wife was there, busy at the kitchen sink, and his daughter was across the table, eating her breakfast and staying quiet. The father said they were used to helping lads who stumbled into their village after being released from prison, it was a regular occurrence. They were the lucky ones, he said – because often, they'd come across lads out in the middle of nowhere, some of them in really bad shape. One had broken his ankle tripping over the stony ground in the dark; another had run into a group of Israeli settlers and been beaten up, left to die; others suffered hypothermia from being outdoors all night.

"Then he told me that just two days before, they'd found the lifeless body of a young man in their neighbour's field. There were no visible signs of injury, so they didn't know how he'd died. But that must have been my friend from Hebron – he never made it home.

"The father asked me where I came from and said that when his son got back for lunch later, they'd both drive me home to Aida. And that's what happened. I didn't know the family was still doing it today, helping lads get home. And now they've been firebombed as punishment. The teenage son I met is dead and the mother and father are in intensive care. The daughter's okay, I've been told. She's married and living in another part of the village." Mohammed pauses. "We need to do everything we can to help this family and their village, we need to give them our support."

"Of course, we'll help them any way we can," says Caleb, "but we also need to look into what's happening at that prison. I can't believe they just turn prisoners out in the middle of the night, with no clue where they are and how they're going to get home. Is that normal?"

"Not at the prison where I worked," says Samuel, picking up the conversation. "The family gets notified when a prisoner is being released and they're usually there to meet them at the gate. But this prison's a small one in the middle of nowhere, and it's operating practically off the grid. It might be for juveniles, but it's got a reputation for being one of the harshest in the West Bank."

"Ice must really have had it in for you, Hassan, getting you locked up there!" Eva says. "I bet you wish you'd had a guard like Samuel looking out for you!"

"Speaking of which," Caleb says, turning to Samuel, "how's Omar doing? Did you get to talk to him as you'd hoped?"

Samuel nods. "We had a good chat on my last night when I went to say my goodbyes. For what it's worth, he said he'd think about coming to one of our meetings when he gets out, but that's still four years away and god knows where his head will be by then. My best advice is to forget about him for now, there's nothing more you can do."

Caleb knows this; he wasn't really expecting Samuel to have anything more positive for him, but he still feels a tug of disappointment. He was foolish to think Omar might have used Samuel's retirement as an opportunity to say something more concrete, to maybe have given Samuel a letter to pass on to Caleb in reply to his own, sent so many years ago. Caleb turns away, looks out the window. "Hey, we're here," he says, spotting some houses up ahead. "There's the village."

When the minibus comes to a stop, Hassan makes his way toward the centre of the village ready to join the funeral procession, leaving the others to unload the minibus and get things set up in the field for the vigil later. They've brought tarpaulin, struts and ropes to erect awnings to keep everyone protected from the sun; five-gallon chilled water containers and stacks of paper cups; rugs to sit on; first-aid kits; everything they can think of to help care for the villagers this afternoon. There's no sign of Israeli settlers hanging around yet, but the army jeeps are there, parked further up the road, just waiting. "I hope those guys are going to behave today," Caleb says, nodding toward them.

"They'd better!" Reuben says, with a force that takes Caleb by surprise. "That's my son over there!"

Caleb squints at the soldiers, trying to make out their features, but it's difficult from this distance – they all look the same. "Are you sure?" he says.

"Yes, that's definitely him!" Reuben replies, sounding anxious. "And he's the one in charge – the commander." Reuben pauses, takes a breath. "This is the first time since joining Combatants United that I've run into him out here. I'm not sure what to expect, how he's going to act, whether I should be worried."

"It's certainly a strange situation to be in," Caleb says, "but he's your son and I've no doubt he follows your example. He's not going to be like some of the other commanders we see, attacking the Palestinian people when they should be peacekeeping."

"I've got no idea what he'll do!" Reuben says. "His sister was killed by a suicide bomber nine years ago and now he's in command of his own army unit. The two of us have taken separate paths in the healing process, and I don't know where he is on his – he still won't talk about it."

"Well," Caleb says, "today is the day you find out."

By early afternoon, Caleb and the others have got everything set up for the vigil and they're sitting under an awning, resting, when they see the villagers begin to make their way across the road toward the field. "Looks like the funerals are over," Caleb says, scrambling to his feet. The soldiers are out of their jeeps now, he sees. They're standing in the next field, relaxed and talking among themselves. Caleb wonders which one is Reuben's son – it's not clear who's in charge. Then he notices them stop talking and turn in the direction of the neighbouring settlement. Caleb pivots to look in the same direction, and then sees them too. A group of settlers are walking through the field in their direction, and they're armed with rifles, sticks and knives.

Caleb turns to the soldiers and sees one of them talking urgently to the others, issuing orders. "Your son?" he asks Reuben. The reply comes back as a whisper: "Yes."

There's a lot of animated discussion among the soldiers, and now they're picking up their rifles, slinging them over their shoulders, getting ready to move. *What has Reuben's son ordered them to do?* Caleb wonders. *Surely not to join the attack! Defend the villagers? Or assume a neutral peacekeeping role?* The soldiers are on the move. They form a line across the field, then turn to face the settlers and aim their guns in the air. The settlers come to a stop. *Now what?* All eyes are on the commander, Reuben's son.

"Go home!" he shouts at the settlers. "Leave this to us."

"This is our business too!" one of the settlers shouts back, to the noisy approval of the others, and they begin walking forward again, narrowing the gap between themselves and the soldiers. Reuben's son quickly marches up to the ringleader, grabs him by the arm and manhandles him toward two of his team, who frogmarch him away and throw him into the back of a jeep. Reuben's son shouts to the other settlers, "Anyone else want a trip to the cells?"

Slowly, they begin to turn around and walk away, back in the direction they came from. The soldiers go across to where the villagers are assembled at the side of the field, and they start leading them toward the vigil spot where Caleb and the others are ready to receive them with cups of chilled water. Reuben's son sees an elderly woman stumble and rushes to help her up, supports her under the elbow until two of the village men come across and take her from him.

"That's what we mean when we say we must 'influence from within'!" Samuel says. "What a fine young man you've raised, Reuben."

Reuben's got tears in his eyes as he watches his son in action for the first time.

"I wish I'd had a commander who'd practised that kind of de-escalation," Caleb says, clasping Reuben's shoulder. "What an incredible difference it makes."

17

Omar

Omar keeps his attention fixed on Caleb, his face inscrutable, as Caleb informs the audience how, as a youngster, he'd been told that when his predecessors arrived on these shores, it had been "a land without a people for a people without a land" and that it had never occurred to him to see this as fake news, to wonder where the Palestinians had come from, and that maybe they'd already been there, squeezed aside and then out to make room for more arriving Israelis. The year 1948 saw the creation of Israel, when so many Palestinians were evicted from their villages and pushed across the newly declared borders into what is left of Palestine today. Then the Six Day War in 1967 marked the start of the Occupation. Everyone thought it was just a temporary state of affairs, that the Israelis would turn around and reverse out some stage soon. But no. A new breed of Israeli Zionist emerged who thought it their life's mission to put down roots and claim the West Bank as a rightful extension of Israel, and from there the current-day settlements have bloomed, and that's considered by many to be a good thing. "It's strange, to realise you don't think the same way as your family and the community you grew up in," Caleb says, "that their truth is so very different from your own."

Omar can't take it any longer: he has to look away, to seek out Eva. She's still standing with the production crew off to one side. Over the past few weeks she's been completely immersed in the task of getting the best possible coverage of this evening's event. She's smiling, looking happy with how it's all going, and Omar is pleased for her. He can remember the moment he first laid eyes on this woman three years ago. He'd known immediately he was in trouble: him Palestinian, her Israeli. Utter madness. Doomed to end in disaster. He should have steered clear, but it was that laugh, and those boots...

September 2019 – Flags and the Flute

Omar has been keeping watch on the doorway since he arrived a little under an hour ago. He's on edge, breathless from dread, steeling himself for Caleb Levy to make an appearance. So when she emerges through the doorway, he's completely blind-sided. She's carrying a tray of poster paints. It's a windy day, and the brightly coloured bottles are toppling over like skittles. She laughs as she props them back up, and does a little curtsy to her group when she has them all back under control. She's dressed entirely in black. He's used to seeing women dressed in black, sure he is, but not like this: black jeans, black T-shirt, black leather jacket, black biker boots. She's an astonishing sight.

Omar's mother had been bending his ear just this morning about finding a good woman and settling down, now that he was home again. "Your rogue days are behind you now, and you're no longer a young man," she'd said, "but you're lucky because Farah is still keen on you and she lives right here in Khaybar."

"It'd be like marrying my sister!" Omar had protested. "We grew up with each other! We shared the same bath!"

"So? What's your problem? That girl has been waiting for you to come home all these years! You owe it to her. Think how easy it will be when the babies start to come along. Both families are right here, ready to help."

By this stage, Omar was struggling to keep his irritation in check. "Mother, please! Enough! You know I want to settle down, but not yet. I'm not ready, so tell Farah and her mother to look elsewhere."

"Not ready? What do you mean, 'not ready'?"

"I've got unfinished business I need to attend to first. You know that."

"What unfinished business, Omar?" his mother had tutted. "You mean the Israelis? You still think you need to solve that? Getting married and starting a family; that's your only unfinished business now. The Israelis weren't attacking you that day, they were attacking all of us, and our problem with them is never going to be over. Give up, Omar."

It's not the first time he's had this conversation with his mother since he returned home six weeks ago. "Put it all behind you", "settle down", "make do", "be satisfied": this has been his mother's advice. But not enough has changed during the fourteen years he's been away for any of that to be possible. A generator, donated by a Danish NGO, has brought power to Khaybar at last, so they've now got refrigerators and televisions, electric lights and cookers. Big deal! Meanwhile, the settlement at the top of the hill has expanded and new rows of houses are marching their way down the hillside toward them, accommodating a growing population of hostile Israelis for neighbours.

"It's time to pass the problem on to the younger ones to deal with," his mother had claimed this morning.

"What 'younger ones'?" he'd replied. "They've all left! And I don't blame them! That's the choice now, isn't it – leave to find work, either with the Israelis, or overseas if you're lucky, or stay and wait for charitable handouts from the international community."

Omar's right, and his mother knows it. There are no Palestinian employers to work for out here in Area C anymore: they've had their factories shut down by the Israeli authorities, and their agriculture sabotaged by Israeli settlers.

"Look how that quarry set up by the rich Palestinian man living in Dubai was closed by the Israeli government, all because it was competing with their own quarry down the road. The one they built on our land!" Omar had continued. "What choice did those workers have, but to go and work for the Israelis? And how about Uncle Yousef? His restaurant was forced out of business when the Israelis blocked its entrance with a ton of cement. Uncle Yousef nearly got himself bulldozed into the ground trying to stop them. They're making it harder and harder for us to stay here in Palestine, determined to force us out one way or another."

"Don't change the subject, Omar."

"I'm not! This is exactly the issue! Should we just put up with what's being done to us? Do you really expect me to settle down in a cave and close my eyes to what's going on around me?"

It was at this point in the conversation this morning that Omar had been rescued by his sister, who'd come running in waving her phone in his direction. "Call for you," she'd said, handing him her mobile.

The only person he'd given his sister's number to was Samuel, his old prison guard. Samuel had been waiting for him outside the prison gates last week when he got released and had driven Omar home to Khaybar. "I promised I'd be waiting for you, so here I am," he'd said simply. Later that day, as Samuel was leaving the Caves, he'd reminded Omar that he too had made a promise during their last meeting four years ago: "You said you'd think about coming along to a Combatants United meeting when you were free, maybe talking to Caleb. So how about it?"

"Sure, let's see," Omar had replied, and he'd given Samuel his sister's number to be contacted on. He hadn't expected to receive a call so soon. The guy on the phone had introduced himself as Hassan, the Palestinian coordinator of Combatants United. "I believe Samuel told you about us? We're a group of Israeli and Palestinian activists, working together to confront the Occupation through peaceful resistance." Whatever – Caleb is a member and Omar knows it's time to confront him. If Caleb's bullet hadn't ricocheted and hit him in the head that day, his life wouldn't have been thrown so violently sideways, but now he's got the chance to steer things to a close: his "unfinished business".

"I hear you're handy with a paint brush and can play a tune on the flute," Hassan had said on the phone. "We could use your help this afternoon."

The immediacy of "this afternoon" had put Omar's head into a spin. So soon? Was he really ready for this? Today? But he'd made a promise to himself back in prison: if he ever got the chance to address his demons, to straighten things out, he'd take it. "Sure! What's going on?" he'd replied.

"We're staging a re-enactment of the 1967 United Nations Resolution over at the Wall," Hassan said. "To protest the Israeli Prime Minister's planned annexation of the Jordan Valley and to remind the world that the Occupation is unlawful. All our members are taking part, and we've got media coverage arranged too. We're hoping to grab international attention with this. We're all meeting at the El Capitan Hotel first, to make the flags. We could do with your artistic skills to help us out."

All our members included Caleb, Omar realised. *He* was going to be there! "I'd be happy to help," he'd replied.

"And then this evening, over at the Wall, it would be great if you could lead the Palestinian procession with your flute. Play something traditional, patriotic, help create the right atmosphere, if you know what I mean."

"I've got the perfect tune," Omar had replied, his excitement building. The fact that he only knew how to play one tune, and that it might not be one hundred percent perfect for the occasion, wasn't something he was going to worry Hassan about – Samuel had obviously recommended him for the role, and he knew that Omar's repertoire was limited. Yes, it was all going to be fine. "My flute and I will see you this afternoon," he'd told Hassan.

He's thought about his long-suffering family and friends, who've all stuck with him through his life-threatening injury at the hands of an Israeli soldier and his not-so-peaceful resistance to the Occupation afterward. Some will say he's not fully recovered from his injury, that his head's still not right, if he's even considering the idea of joining a peace organisation alongside Israelis. They simply won't believe him, they'll doubt the sincerity of his intentions. Others will accuse him of "consorting with the enemy", of "normalising the Occupation", of being no different from those Palestinians who've found work in the Israeli factories and fields. How can they come together as equals, when the Palestinians' need for peace is so much more urgent than the Israelis'? That's what they'll say. But it's only through Combatants United that Omar can reach Caleb. His family and friends will come to understand in the end.

So here he is this afternoon, at the El Capitan Hotel, drawing the outlines of the Canadian maple leaf, the Indian spoked wheel and the Soviet sickle and hammer onto fabric sheets ready for the painters to colour in. The dozen or so Israelis in the group have entered the West Bank at the Separation Wall crossing and they'll return back the same way later, taking the group's effort at the State of Israel flag with them.

"Finished already?" Hassan comes up behind Omar, catching him unaware.

"Hmm? Oh, yes, all done."

"Fast work. You can come again!" Hassan says, but Omar's too distracted to reply. His full attention is focused on the far side of the courtyard. It's where that stunning Israeli woman is now sitting, with Samuel and five other people. Judging from the lively conversation and laughter around their table, they must be pretty good friends. She's working on one of the flags, he sees, dipping her brush into red paint and daubing it across the fabric. *Is that the Canadian flag she's working on?* Omar wonders. He hopes she's paying attention and keeping inside the lines he's so carefully drawn. Dare he go over and take a look?

"That's Eva, by the way," Hassan says, following Omar's gaze. "One of our Israeli members. She was once a journalist, but now she's our full-time Communications Officer." He pats Omar on the shoulder and moves on to the next table.

Eva sits back to survey her work, her expression intense, critical. Her hair is cut into a sharp, chin-length bob, black and sleek. In that moment she looks austere, reminding Omar of those lifelike avatars you see exhibited at technology shows. But then she smiles and tucks her hair behind her ear, and any resemblance to a robot is gone. She glances his way and catches his eye. Is that a spark of recognition? But the moment passes, and she turns back to talk to her neighbour. He's sure she recognised him, but how? From where? They haven't met before, he's certain of that.

As he continues watching, Omar sees her attention get drawn suddenly to her phone, and she snatches it up from the table with a frown. Who is she talking to? It looks serious. She rummages through a satchel that's slung on the back of her chair, and grabs a notebook. She opens it and starts writing. The conversation lasts no longer than a minute, then she hangs up, gathers her things and gets up from the table, waving goodbye to the others. After she's gone he can't help feeling deflated, like she's taken all the buzz of the afternoon with her. Everyone else, though, is just carrying on as they were: painting, chatting, laughing, Israelis and Palestinians together, relaxed like it's an everyday occurrence. He's never experienced anything quite like this.

Once all the flags are finished, the Israelis in the group depart, taking their one blue-and-white flag with them. "Six o'clock sharp – don't be late!" Hassan shouts after them, jokingly. They shake their heads and wave dismissively. "Right back at you!" one of them shouts in reply. Hassan turns to Omar, grinning. "We're late for everything," he says. "Drives them crazy."

"Caleb Levy's not with them?" Omar's trying to sound casual, but the question comes out a little too strangled for that.

Hassan shakes his head. "No, but he'll be joining us at the Wall later," he says, frowning. "Look, I know you and Caleb have history, but this isn't going to be a problem, is it?" he asks. "We can't have friction in the group, settling of old scores, that's not what we're about. You understand that, right?"

"Yes, of course," Omar says. "Samuel and I talked about this a lot during our time together in prison. It was him who suggested I come along, meet with Caleb. Don't worry, my intentions are good."

Hassan nods, ending the conversation. "Come on," he says, "let's get the flags loaded onto the van. We can't keep our friends waiting."

Fifteen minutes later, the convoy of Palestinian vehicles is making its way along rutted dirt tracks toward the Wall. Omar is squeezed in the back of Hassan's van, sharing the confined space with their fifteen newly made flags and willing the journey to end: the smell of fresh paint is not helping with his motion sickness and he's not sure how long he can hold out. Hassan's at the wheel, and another veteran member of Combatants United, Mohammed, is in the passenger seat. They've both got their windows wound down for Omar's sake, but it's letting in far more dust than air. Hassan's got the radio turned up loud, tuned to a local Palestinian station. The music is interrupted for the news, and they all listen closely to the latest coming out of Israel:

With Israelis going to the polls tomorrow for the second general election this year, tensions on both sides of the Wall are rising. After failing to gain enough seats in the April elections to form a government, and with insufficient support from rival parties to form a coalition, the Prime Minister's latest strategy is to sway the Israeli electorate with promises of more annexation of Palestinian lands. He has pledged that if he wins the general election tomorrow, he will immediately annex the Jordan Valley to Israel, along with all the Israeli settlements in the West Bank. This move is being presented as the first step toward implementation of the so-called "deal of the century" promulgated recently by the United States...

"That's more than a fifth of the land we have left," Hassan grumbles. "Haven't they taken enough already? Why do they need more? They built Israel on land that was once ours, and now they want the rest."

...The United Nations has denounced the move, saying that any attempt by Israel to annex further Palestinian territory would be unlawful under international law...

"The UN's been saying that since 1967, when Israel first established military occupation over Palestine. What good does it ever do?" Hassan stabs his finger at the radio, silencing it. "Israel will continue to do exactly what it wants, as long as it has the support of its big brother, the United States."

"Most of the world has no idea, even, that Palestine still exists," Mohammed says. "People think it's all the same thing – that it's all Israel – and that Palestine is some long-lost civilization, like Babylonia or Phoenicia. Almost mythical. In which case, what are we – dodos?"

"That's why we're here today, though, isn't it?" Omar says. "To remind the world we still exist, and that we want our independence back."

"You're right," says Mohammed, turning around and glancing at Omar. "I'm looking forward to what we've got planned today – and our timing couldn't be better."

"I'm not sure about that, at least not on our part," Hassan says, grinning and pointing to a spot up ahead. "Our Israeli colleagues are here already. We're late, again!"

Omar shifts his position to get a better view. In this rural stretch of the border, the Separation Wall has given way to two parallel lines of post-and-wire fencing, with a tarmac road running along the no-man's land in between. Up ahead, on the Israeli side, Omar spots a blue-and-white flag flapping above the heads of a huddled group: their Israeli comrades. The Israelis have brought the media, their vans positioned off to the side, and this unusual activity has brought out the Israeli army; there are three armoured jeeps parked on the no-man's land, sitting tight.

As Omar leads the procession up to the fence, he makes quite the pied piper with his flute and bright red and green plumed hat (the fact it's in Marzen's colours being just coincidence). Hassan is following closely behind, banging the beat of Omar's tune on his drum. Then come all the standard-bearers, waving their flags in a vivid kaleidoscope of colour and chanting at the tops of their voices: *Peace! Freedom! Dignity! Peace! Freedom! Dignity!* Meanwhile, there's quite the welcoming committee awaiting them at the meeting point. The soldiers have got out of their jeeps and are standing ready, hands on rifles; and the Israeli Combatants United members are shouting at the soldiers through the fence, telling them their presence is not required and to go home. It's a scene made for news, and the cameras are rolling.

Reaching the meeting point, the Palestinians come to a standstill. Their music and chanting stops and silence descends. They face their Israeli counterparts across the narrow strip of no-man's land, avoiding eye contact with the soldiers that stand, fenced in, between them. Omar spots Samuel, his old prison guard, and gives him a nod. Caleb's over there too, the man of Omar's nightmares, right there in the flesh. When he catches Caleb's eye, Omar feels a spark of satisfaction to see him flinch.

Hassan lifts his megaphone and breaks the silence:

"We, the United Nations Security Council, assembled on this day, November 22nd, 1967, call upon the Member States present to approve the following resolutions. First, the withdrawal of Israeli armed forces from territories occupied in the recent conflict; and second, termination of all claims or states of belligerency and respect for and acknowledgement of the sovereignty, territorial integrity and political independence of every State in the area and their right to live in peace within secure and recognized boundaries free from threats or acts of force."

Hassan passes the megaphone to Mohammed, who's stepped forward to stand next to him.

"How do you all vote?" Mohammed demands, turning to face the assembled Palestinians. "China?"

"China votes Yes!" they all shout back. "Israel must end the Occupation now!" and the bright red flag of China gets swooped from side-to-side.

The process is repeated through each of the other Member States of the UN Security Council that voted on this resolution back in 1967: France? United Kingdom? United States? Soviet Union? Argentina? Brazil? Bulgaria? Canada? Denmark? Ethiopia? India? Japan? Mali? Nigeria? As it was then, the vote is again: unanimous. For each and every Member State, there's the same enthusiastic sweep of its flag, the same loud and clear answer in the affirmative from the assembled Palestinians: *Yes! Yes! Yes!* Across the way, the Israelis look on, silent and still; in the no-man's land that separates them, the soldiers stand watchful, gripping their rifles; off to the side, the cameras pan, capturing it all on film.

Mohammed turns to face the Israelis, lifts his megaphone. "Representatives of Israel here today, do you respect this resolution of the UN Security Council?"

There's no response from the Israelis, they just stand in silence. A few are looking in the Palestinians' direction, but most are looking down at their feet.

"Israel, we ask you again: do you accept that you must end the Occupation of the Palestinian territories and withdraw to your side of the pre-1967 line?"

Tension is building as the silent seconds tick by. The soldiers are getting twitchy and most of them have started pacing backward and forward along the length of the two fences.

Mohammed raises the megaphone again. "Israel, we need your answer!"

Omar sees that it's Eva who's carrying the flag of Israel. She's facing the soldiers, fixing them with a defiant stare. Two others go to join her, it's Caleb and Samuel, and together they raise the flag high into the air.

"Israel!" Mohammed demands again, louder this time, more urgent. "How do you respond?"

The Israelis are watching Eva, waiting for her signal. She says nothing, just gives a nod, and they all turn their backs to the Palestinians and walk away, led by Eva, Samuel and Caleb and the blue-and-white flag.

Although this was exactly what the group had discussed earlier at the hotel – a turning of Israeli backs on the collective will of the United Nations – to Omar it feels like a personal rejection, all too true to life: a real slap in the face. It's irrational, he knows, but he feels sickened by it. He, too, turns his back and walks away.

18

Eva

Eva notices Omar looking her way and she smiles, gives him a wink. She knows he's still a conundrum to many of her friends in Combatants United, that they don't fully trust him, but she decided some time ago to believe the best of him. Yes, he's a bit of a rebel, he has the remnants of a wild past about him but, for her, that's a large part of the attraction. And he's a decent, funny guy under that cool exterior. She enjoys hanging out with him at the Combatants United events, even flirting with him a little. But dating? That's a total non-starter. Think of the practicalities! They wouldn't be able hold down any kind of serious relationship even if that's what they both wanted. She's Israeli and not permitted to live in Palestine other than in a settlement. He's a West Bank Palestinian and not permitted to live in a settlement or in Israel. Their options are mutually exclusive, a future together is impossible – which is why she knows she can daydream in safety.

Caleb is finishing his speech, thanking the audience for coming along this evening, for tuning in remotely – they're all stars, he tells them. Hassan steps forward and they both raise their hands, acknowledging the applause that's spreading through the arena. People start to stand and the clapping swells louder. Hassan turns to Caleb and puts his arm around his shoulder. Caleb reciprocates. *What a fantastic job they've done as opening speakers*, Eva thinks, *the audience is enthralled and they both look so pleased.* She's delighted for them.

It's Reuben and Mohammed next. Eva sees Reuben take Mohammed by the arm, ready to make their way forward to the stage. But she suddenly notices Omar, too, as he brushes past them and turns their smiles into looks of confusion. Omar is walking quickly now, toward the steps at the side of the stage. Hassan and Caleb haven't noticed him yet, they're still at the microphone together, waving happily to the audience. Now Omar's on the stage and he's making a beeline for the two men, his attention completely focused on them and oblivious to all else. *What the hell..?*

September 2019 – In Search of Better Coffee

Eva is running her critical eye over the new guy's work. It's the outline of a maple leaf, executed cleanly and with precision. *Nice*, she thinks. Now it's her job to turn it into the Canadian flag with the help of some poster paint and she's feeling an unexpected pressure not to mess it up. *Why did Canada's founders choose the colour of blood for their flag, anyway?* she wonders. *They could have chosen anything – blue for the water, green for the forests, orange for the sun, but bright red?* She looks up from her work, and catches the new guy staring at her from across the courtyard. She hasn't seen him at any of the Combatants United meetings before, but still, there's something familiar about him. That scarring on his cheek: not something you'd easily forget. Has she seen him some place before? The way he's staring at her is like he, too, is trying to place how they know each other. She turns to Samuel, sitting next to her and absorbed with painting a pleasing orange stripe across his own flag. "Who's that guy over there, looking this way? He seems familiar – I'm sure we've crossed paths somewhere."

"I doubt it," says Samuel. "That's Omar. He's the Palestinian that Caleb injured years ago over in Khaybar. He was with the Palestinian police for a while, but went rogue soon after that, joined an extremist group and ended up doing time in prison. I got to know him quite well in there – I was one of his guards. He was released just last week and is trying to find his feet."

Of course, that's why he looks so familiar – it's Caleb's guy! She recognises him now, from the picture that had appeared in the liberal newspapers back in 2005: the Palestinian policeman stumbling under the weight of his dead friend, his scarred and tear-stained face the epitome of anguish. Her colleague, Tamar, had covered the story and had gone to Khaybar to interview his mother about him joining the police after he'd been injured by the Israeli army. She'd loaned Tamar some photos of him from happier times, and when Eva had seen them, she'd joked with Tamar that it was a pity all the good-looking guys were Palestinian: off-limits; out of bounds; taboo. Even if you were crazy enough to date one of them, where could you go without being stared at as if you were committing some heinous crime? No, she's stayed well clear of all that, thank you very much. In fact, it's not only Palestinian men she's given a wide berth, but all men in general. She's tried holding down relationships in the past, even lived with a guy for a while, but in the end her career has always driven them away. She's been accused of being a workaholic, an extreme ideologue, and everything in between. Nowadays she sticks to one-night stands, it's easier that way. She's the Communications Officer for Combatants United, and there's no room in her life for much else.

She'd like to quiz Samuel some more, about Omar's time in prison and what's brought him to the El Capitan Hotel today, but her phone starts to ring. It's the journalist from News Twenty-Four, the Israeli television channel. He tells her they're at the Wall and need her to come and brief them on what to expect later. She scribbles a note, a reminder to follow up on Omar when she's back at her desk next week. "It's showtime, people, the media has arrived to cover our demonstration," she says, getting up from the table. "See you all at the meeting point at six."

Later that afternoon, they're being asked by megaphone from the other side of no-man's land if they're in favour of the United Nations resolution to end the Occupation. The Israeli flag is heavy, and Samuel and Caleb are helping her to hold it steady. Eva knows what she needs to do – they've got it all planned out to make this moment the most dramatic possible for the cameras – but now that the time has come, it suddenly feels cruel, turning their backs on their Palestinian partners. The tension is building and all eyes are on her. She's fixing the soldiers with her fiercest stare, willing them to restrain themselves. Beyond them, across the two fences, she sees Omar standing next to Hassan, waiting for her answer.

Mohammed demands again through his megaphone: "Israel! How do you respond?"

"It's time," Eva says to Samuel and Caleb. "Don't forget to sneer for the cameras."

When they turn and walk away, Eva can't help herself: she looks over her shoulder, but Omar is already leaving.

A week later, Eva has arranged to meet Omar at the Combatants United office in Bethlehem. He's the organisation's newest member, and it's her job to interview him to get his life story, ready to post on their website along with everyone else's. As usual, she's come across the border on her motorbike. Not so usual is the makeup bag she's brought with her. When she arrives, she heads straight to the washroom to "freshen up" instead of going to the kitchen for coffee and a chat with whoever's around. He's an unknown quantity, this one, and a dash of red lipstick will armour her far better than a weak shot of caffeine.

When she makes her way into the meeting room, Omar is already there, sitting at the table. He rises slightly as she enters, and she notices the colour run up his neck and into his face, causing the star-shaped scar below his eye to stand out in white relief.

"Good morning! Sorry I'm late! You must be Omar!" She puts on her friendliest, most welcoming smile and holds out her hand. Omar seems to remember he's got legs and springs forward to take it, shaking it enthusiastically. He looks around the room with a grim expression. "No offence, but I'm told the coffee here is awful, and prison mats are more comfortable than these seats," he says, and she detects the start of a grin, softening his features. "Shall we go somewhere else?" he asks. "There's a café down the road that should be quiet this time of the day. I'm sure you'd like it."

He's not wrong about their coffee (it's that filtered stuff you find in work canteens everywhere: watery, lukewarm and generally nasty) but nonetheless, she feels a prickle of worry over Omar's suggestion they change venues. Omar and Caleb still haven't spoken, let alone met face-to-face, despite Caleb's attempts to reach him since their demonstration at the Wall last week. "I don't think he'll be offering the hand of friendship any time soon," is Caleb's verdict. Not even Samuel, Omar's biggest champion in the group, has been able to add much more, only that he'd been "heading in the right direction four years ago". The guy's motives for joining them are, at best, unproven. There's also the issue of the Marzen anthem. Hassan has told her that's what Omar was playing on his flute last week when he led the procession to the Wall. He couldn't stop him, he said – the cameras were rolling and he didn't want to draw attention to what was being played, so he'd kept going, following along behind Omar and beating his drum. "I wondered why you were looking so uncomfortable," Eva told him, "but at least nobody was singing the words – then we'd have been in real trouble."

She's re-watched the footage from that day a couple of times. That swagger, the hat in Marzen's distinctive red and green, the anger on his face the moment the Israelis turned their backs and walked away. She's also tried to do some background research on him online, but it didn't turn up anything she didn't already know. His twelve years in prison are a complete blackout. Before that, a short article in one of the mainstream newspapers reporting his conviction and prison sentence, alongside a photo of him in police uniform. The caption: "Even the Palestinian police are terrorists".

Eva's looking at Omar, weighing him up. "Come on, we're both on the same side now, remember!" he says, and she has to admit, he does seem friendly enough, charming even.

"Yes, of course we're on the same side," Eva replies. "It's just that I'm not supposed to be here in Bethlehem – it's an Area A town, isn't it? Our Israeli members take enough of a risk coming to the office. I have to keep a low profile this side of the border."

He looks her up and down. "Hmm, I like your idea of a low profile," he says, raising an eyebrow. "You blend in perfectly with all the other women in biker's leathers this side of the Wall."

Eva feels her hackles rise. "Lead the way," she says, turning on her heel and walking out the door, leaving Omar scrambling to catch up with her.

When they reach the café, they find a free table in the far corner and Omar gets them both coffees from the counter. As soon as he's seated, she switches on her recorder and asks him straight out, "Why did you play the Marzen anthem at the demonstration the other day?"

"Because it's the only tune I know how to play all the way through," he replies. "I learned it during my time with Marzen." Eva takes a sip of her coffee and looks at him, keeping her expression neutral. "Am I under investigation here?" he asks. "Maybe I should have brought my lawyer." He chuckles and reaches for his own coffee.

"Sorry, no!" Eva says, shaking her head. "No lawyers required. Please, start at the beginning and tell me your story."

So he tells her about being injured in Khaybar by a bullet that had ricocheted off the ground; his time in hospital where he met a policeman and decided to join up himself; his friend being shot and killed; then going off to join Marzen and ending up in prison – what he describes as a "transformative experience". Then he tells her about Samuel meeting him at the prison gates when he was released just a few weeks ago, and then finally, getting a call from Hassan, asking him along to a Combatants United event.

"Wow, that's quite a journey!" Eva finds Omar's candidness, the fact he's willing to open up about the bad things in his past as well as the good, reassuring. "What was your role in Marzen?" she asks. She's digging a bit more than she should, but she's trying to get a feel for the man, whether his claim that he's on a non-violent path nowadays is plausible. "Were you on the front lines or working behind the scenes?"

Omar seems unfazed with the line of questioning. "Apart from targeting people working on the Israeli settlement near Khaybar, which as you know got me arrested, I left all the macho stuff to the others. I helped with logistics, mainly. I sourced explosives, trained activists how to use them, thing like that."

"By *activists*, you mean suicide bombers?"

"That's right," Omar replies. "In fact, I helped one of the few female suicide bombers with her mission. She was a brave, determined lady."

Eva suddenly feels sick. She's already certain of the answer, but makes herself ask anyway. "Heba El-Issa?"

Omar looks at her quizzically.

"I knew Heba! She was a friend of mine," Eva explains. She goes on to tell Omar the story of their friendship, from their very first meeting in the Square in 1995, through to her shock of seeing what Heba had done on the news.

"Our life stories are incredible, aren't they?" Omar says once Eva has finished. "You really couldn't make this stuff up." He sits back then and crosses his arms. "And now, after all that's happened to us, here we are," he says.

"Yes, here we are," Eva replies, wondering where, exactly, Omar thinks that is.

It's time to end the interview, but there's one final point Eva wants to cover. "Off the record: you know Caleb is a member of Combatants United, and he's been trying to talk to you?" she says. "Why haven't you met with him yet?"

"I'm waiting for the right moment," Omar replies.

19

Omar

Present Day – Millennium Arena, Tel Aviv

Omar has made it onto the stage. He's nearly to the mic. His heart is thudding in his chest, making him breathless, lightheaded. He's suddenly got the jitters, but it's too late to stop now; he can't just turn around, go back down the steps, return to his seat. No, he's got to keep going, see it through.

Across the arena, the thunderous din of Hassan and Caleb's standing ovation just a few moments ago has given way to the eerie buzz of a thousand whispers. Omar knows everyone's wondering what's going on, whether they should be worried. He glances quickly at the audience and mouths an apology. He can see Eva. She's got her hand clamped over her mouth, and her eyes, wide with surprise, are tracking him across the stage. He's bursting for her to know she's got nothing to worry about, that whatever happens this evening, it will be okay.

His original idea was to use this moment to finally address Caleb. After such a long wait, he should give the guy something extra special, make a real splash. But then the more he thought about it, the bigger it became: the idea that he could use this moment for something far more ambitious, to deliver the most powerful blow possible to all those who work at keeping them divided.

He reaches the spot in the centre of the stage where Hassan and Caleb are standing. They're both watching him in puzzlement. Hassan's expression is one of amused curiosity; he knows Omar well enough not to be worried. Caleb, on the other hand, is looking far more nervous. "Sorry to keep you hanging," Omar tells him. "Please, just one moment longer."

Omar stands behind the mic, gives it a tap, clears his throat and steadies his gaze. "Good evening ladies and gentlemen! I apologise for interrupting this evening's program, but I have something important to say and I'd be very grateful if you'd allow me a minute to speak," he begins. "I'm the guy that Caleb's says he's been waiting to hear from for a long time. I'm the guy who got injured by Caleb's bullet at Khaybar Caves." He turns to Caleb. "I want you to know that I forgive you, my friend, wholeheartedly and without any reservations." The audience starts to clap, but Omar puts up his hand, silencing them. "Sorry, I have not yet finished what I've come up here to say." He turns to where Eva is standing at the side of the arena, pulls the mic from the stand, and drops to one knee. The audience gasps and a *whoosh* echoes across the arena as ten thousand people suck in their breath. "Eva," he says, "will you marry me?"

EPILOGUE

Six Months Later

It's one of those beautiful clear winter evenings Palestine is so often blessed with. A luminous white crescent moon is hanging lazily in the chilly sky, backdropped by a million twinkling stars. It's a perfect night for a celebration in the courtyard of the El Capitan Hotel.

Mohammed and Samuel are sitting together with their wives, chatting like it's the old days, except now Reuben and his wife have joined them too. Caleb, the best man, is off somewhere rehearsing his speech and trying to get his nerves under control. A gong sounds from inside the hotel and Hassan comes marching into the courtyard, banging his drum to the beat of the Marzen anthem and causing everyone to laugh. Then comes the bride and groom, their smiles fit to rival the crescent moon.

Eva and Omar. They married a week ago, alone in Cyprus because neither Israel nor Palestine would do them the honour. Tonight, they are celebrating their union with everyone who wishes to celebrate it with them. It's a small gathering. Eva's family declined their invitation. Omar's family are here, though, happy to see him settle down at long last, even if it's not at the Caves.

They're setting up home together in a Palestinian-Israeli village just outside Tel Aviv. It's all low-key, because Omar doesn't have rights of residency in Israel, and probably never will. But they'll work it out, find a way forward – just look at how far they've already come.

ACKNOWLEDGEMENTS

My sincere thanks to all those who granted me interviews for this book: Hillel Bardin, Osama Eliwat, Tuly Flint, Michal Hochberg, Sulaiman Khatib, Jamil Qassas, Adam Rabia and Avner Wishnitzer (members of *Combatants for Peace*) and Bassam Aramin, Robi Damelin and Rami Elhanan (members of *The Parents Circle-Families Forum*). Your remarkable lives, tireless spirits and devotion to peace are sufficient inspiration to fill not only this novel, but an entire library. May your dreams soon become reality.